P9-BTN-447

RIGHT BEHIND YOU

RIGHT BEHIND YOU

GAIL GILES

LITTLE, BROWN AND COMPANY
New York Boston

Little, Brown and Company

Hachette Book Group USA
237 Park Avenue, New York, NY 10017
Visit our Web site at www.lb-teens.com

First Edition: September 2007

The characters and events portrayed in this book are fictitious. Any similarity to real persons, living or dead, is coincidental and not intended by the author.

The author wishes to acknowledge Ajahn Pannadhammo and Ajahn Kusalo for the Hungry Ghosts passage on page 68.

Library of Congress Cataloging-in-Publication Data

Giles, Gail.
Right behind you : a novel / by Gail Giles.—1st ed.
p. cm.
Summary: After spending four years in a mental institution for murdering a friend in Alaska, fourteen-year-old Kip begins a completely new life in Indiana with his father and stepmother under a different name, but not only has trouble fitting in, he finds there are still problems to deal with from his childhood.
ISBN-13: 978-0-316-16636-2 (hardcover)
ISBN-10: 0-316-16636-7 (hardcover)
[1. Psychotherapy—Fiction. 2. Family problems—Fiction. 3. Interpersonal relations—Fiction. 4. Murder—Fiction. 5. Identity—Fiction. 6. High schools—Fiction. 7. Schools—Fiction. 8. Alaska—Fiction. 9. Indiana—Fiction.] I. Title.
PZ7.G3923Rig 2007
[Fic]—dc22

2007012336

10 9 8 7 6 5 4 3 2

RRD-C

Printed in the United States of America

Always and always and always for Jim Giles and
Josh Jakubik, my heroes. — G.G.

He stood in front of me, soaked by the rain. It sluiced down his face into his eyes and mouth, but he didn't make a move to wipe it away.

He cradled something wrapped in an olive green poncho.

"There are three things you need to know about me," he said.

"First, you don't know my real name.

"Second, I murdered somebody once.

"Third . . . well, maybe this will tell you."

He thrust the poncho forward. "Please read this. All of it. Swear to me you will."

Real name?

Murdered?

"Sam, will you swear you'll read this?"

I nodded. Reflex.

And he was gone. Down the stairs into the dark and rain.

PART I
ALASKA

Chapter 1
WHAT I KNOW

On the afternoon of his seventh birthday, I set Bobby Clarke on fire.

I was nine.

It was all about Bobby's birthday present.

A baseball glove.

Chapter 2
WHAT I THINK I REMEMBER

It surprises people to learn that summer days can get highs of a hundred degrees in the Alaskan interior. And July is fire season. But it was a windless day, so Dad was planning a controlled burn near our cabin to clear the brush. He had let it get out of hand while Mom was sick.

A lot of things had gotten out of hand while Mom was sick.

Me.

Dad.

Aunt Jemma.

We were miles from any real town or even a road that was more than a rutted dirt trail.

Dad was draining all the gas out of the lawn mower into a small pail.

"Why can't we just go get some gas?"

"Stop whining, Kip. There's no wind this morning. It takes a good hour to get to a gas station. If the wind kicks up while we're going to town, we can't get the burn done. We can make do." Dad handed me the pail.

"Take this and pour it into the bucket outside. Don't get any on your clothes. Be quick about it. I still have to drain the snow machine and the generator."

How stupid was it to make a hot day hotter by tending a fire? I was sick of working hard all the time. And I was tired of "making do" the Alaskan way. Being poor. Following Dad's orders. I gave the lawn mower a toe-bruising kick.

Dad laughed. "You get mad at me, you kick the tire, I don't get a bruise, the tire doesn't care, and you're the only one hurting. How's that working for you, Kip?"

As I poured the last pail of gasoline into the bucket, Dad came out of the shed.

"I don't want to fight with you all day, Kip. Lose the attitude."

"My head hurts."

"Your head hurts whenever there's work to be done."

Dad snapped into his "I-*will*-be-obeyed" voice. "You have to get tough to live in the bush. It's not called the last frontier . . ."

I tuned him out. I'd heard the same lecture on hard work a million times, and I was about ready to throw the gasoline on the house so we wouldn't live in the bush anymore.

He stopped his sermon when we heard a car and then saw the dust swirl on our excuse for a road.

"I think it's Aunt Jemma," I said.

Dad's face went so tight I could see lumps where his jaw was. "And she's here for another fuss," Dad said. "The woman won't leave me alone."

Aunt Jemma's rental car bucked to a stop in front of

our cabin. She got out and slammed her door, rounded the back, opened the trunk, and pulled out boxes.

"What the hell does she think she's doing now?"

Dad was kind of whispering to himself, and he sounded like he could throw Aunt Jemma and her car right down our road.

"Stay out here and straighten up the shed for me, Kip."

He slapped his lighter on the hood of our truck and headed toward Aunt Jemma. They were already arguing before they hit the porch. About me again.

My mother died in April and Aunt Jemma had been hammering at Dad since then to let her take me back to "civilization."

As much as I was sick of the Alaskan way, I wasn't sure I was sick of Alaska. And Aunt Jenna's civilization preached nothing but rules to me. It meant leaving the place where I had memories of Mom. It meant leaving Dad, which I couldn't imagine, even if he made me mad.

Aunt Jemma and Dad's arguing made my head hurt. It reminded me of . . . the other arguing. Mom and Dad's. I always thought that was my fault too.

I could hear their voices. Like hail on our cabin's tin roof. Louder, faster, harder.

"Pigheaded . . ."

"My son . . ."

"Lawyer . . ."

"Over my dead body . . ."

"She died because she couldn't get decent medical care in this . . ."

The hollow inside me filled up with red mean. I banged a snow shovel against the wall in the shed to drown out their storming with mine, but the yelling from the house let words pop between the beats of metal against wood.

And then Bobby Clarke trotted up to the doors of the shed.

"Kip, you here? Come out. I want to show you something."

"I got work to do. My dad says to clean up the shed. Go home."

"Come out and see my birthday present. It's the best baseball glove anybody ever had."

I stepped out of the shed to send the little snot on his way. Bobby was waving the glove in front of my face. "My dad gave me a bike, but I don't know how to ride a two-wheeler yet. This is from my mom. She said it will make me the best player on the T-ball team."

The glove was a beauty. The leather was the color of leaves when they first drop to the ground. And it was on Bobby Clarke's hand.

"Nothing can make you a good baseball player," I said. "You can't catch a ball, not even if you had a glove twice that size."

"You're just mad 'cause you're too poor to have a glove." He waved the glove again, taunting me with it. "You don't even have a mom to give you one." He pushed it toward me, then jerked it away.

I glared at the birthday gift from his mother.

My head throbbed as the voices in the house rose.

Bobby shoved the glove toward my face again.

I wanted to ruin it. Ruin the glove. The birthday glove.

I grabbed the bucket. I sloshed the gasoline on the

glove. It splashed all over his arms and shirt and dribbled down his pants. Some even spattered up on his face.

I don't think he knew what I threw on him. He sputtered when he called me a bad name and pulled his hand out of the glove. Cradled it against his chest.

By then I had the lighter.

Had flipped it open.

Had flicked the wheel.

And as soon as I saw the blue spurt of flame . . .

I pitched it at the birthday baseball glove.

Pitched it onto Bobby Clarke.

Chapter 3
WHAT THEY TOLD ME

I have no memory of what happened after that. I know what my father told me. I know what the doctors told me. I've read the newspaper accounts.

But there is a hole of weeks in my life. And the hole starts with the minute Bobby caught fire. My father says that he heard the screams. Mine and Bobby's. His argument with Aunt Jemma was cut short when he looked out the window and saw one writhing child aflame and another frozen child howling. He says it still shames him that his first emotion was relief to see that I was the frozen howler.

He threw Bobby to the ground. Ripped off his own shirt and covered Bobby, burning his own arms. My aunt was phoning the state troopers already.

Miles from a town.

A rough dirt road.

It took a long time for the ambulance to get to the cabin. It took a long time for the ambulance to get to a place where the LifeFlight helicopter could land. It took a long time to fly to Anchorage.

Bobby lived for three days.

When someone remembered to look for me, I was under our truck in fetal position. Dad pulled me out. He says my face was tear streaked but I was no longer crying. My eyes were open but vacant.

I didn't speak for four months.

My age and my psychiatric state made commitment to a mental hospital the only reasonable answer.

I didn't know where I was for weeks anyway.

Dad moved to Anchorage, where I was confined. Somewhere in his files are stacks of legal papers that deal with my case. He hasn't told me much about the therapy that brought me out of my near-catatonic state. It took five weeks for me to respond. Five.

Dad came in my room, and finally I blinked and slid my eyes to his face.

"Hey, Kipper, you back?"

Dad says I closed my eyes and tears ran down my face. He didn't know if he should hug me or call the doctor. He opted for the hug.

There was therapy. Play therapy. Puppet therapy. Art therapy. I did whatever anyone asked me. I took pills; I drew pictures; I looked at the books; I listened; but I didn't speak.

I didn't know what to say.

There were legal reasons to keep me in the hospital. Before I could be released, doctors had to say they understood what I did. That I understood it. A judge had to say I was not a danger to myself or others. And if I wasn't talking this wasn't going to happen.

I turned ten.

Ten.

I should have been in Boy Scouts.

I weighed sixty-two pounds.

I had a loose back tooth.

I had murdered another child.

Chapter 4
WHEN GLOVES EXPLODE

My first words were "Wile E. Coyote."

It was toward the middle of my hour of not talking to The Frown. The shrink had dark floppy hair, a wrinkled-up forehead, and a constant kind of squint behind his wire-rimmed glasses. He wore rolled-back sleeves, propped his tennis shoes on his desk, and read sailing magazines while I sat silently — I guess to show me that he had all the time in the world.

That day I had taken all the wrapped candies out of the plastic container and sorted them by color.

"I get paid whether you talk or not," he said.

I put a red with the other reds.

"Just so you know."

The Frown reached into his bottom drawer and pulled out a Nerf ball and tossed it into a small hoop attached to his closet door. It was made to look like a basketball but was way smaller, about the size of those little black bombs in the cartoons. . . .

"Wile E. Coyote."

My voice surprised me. Rusty. Like the first time we opened the cabin windows in spring.

If The Frown was surprised to hear me after months of nothing, he didn't show it. He shot the ball again. Missed. "The cartoon guy?"

"Yeah."

The Frown put the ball down, but not his feet. "He's cool. The coyote. But he messes up a lot."

I put a green candy with the yellow ones. Looked at The Frown. Waited for him to see the clue. There was something wrong with the picture.

He looked at me and waited. I scooped the candies up

and slammed them into the bowl. I wanted to throw the candy bowl straight at The Frown's head because he was so stupid. I tucked my hands under my thighs instead.

At my next session I sorted the candy and The Frown tapped a pencil against a legal pad.

"The coyote thing — the cartoon guy. I got it wrong?"

"Wile E. Coyote," I said.

"Yeah. You didn't say his name because he messes up a lot. You thought of him for another reason."

I paused in my sorting and looked up at him. "It's not because he messes up." I sorted a few more candies. "I don't know what it's about. Not for sure."

"So give it your best shot, Kip. No right or wrong answers here."

I sat there running the cartoons in my head. The roadrunner with his legs spinning into sort of a blurred wheel. The coyote running off the cliff, his feet pedaling in the air before he drops. Then I saw it again. The picture I needed. "It's about the bomb."

The Frown stopped in mid-tap. "Like when he's holding that round bomb thing with the fuse?"

Something hot clogged my throat but I forced my words through. "Uh-huh, the fuse burns down and the glove explodes and then you see the coyote and he's all smoking and his fur is all burned and his eyes are all big. And everybody laughs because he's gonna be right back chasing the roadrunner bird and his fur won't be burnt anymore."

"The glove explodes?"

"What?" Which one of us was crazy here?

"Glove. You said, 'the glove explodes.'"

"I said *bomb*."

The Frown eased back in his chair and tapped his chin with the pencil. "I'd be expecting to hear you say 'bomb.' That's why the glove thing surprised me."

"I never said 'glove.'" The Frown nodded his head. He looked like one of those Bobblehead dolls. "You need to wash your ears or something," I said.

"You're upset."

"I have a headache," I said. "Can I go?"

"Sure, talk to the nurse. You have orders for pain meds if you need them."

Chapter 5
WHEN PEOPLE EXPLODE

My home — or the "hood," as the older kids called it — was a "state mental ward for dangerous juvenile offenders." The ward was supposed to be for twelve- to fourteen-year-olds. At nine, I was the youngest to enter for the four years and seven months I lived there. Before me, there had been no provisions for under-twelves that committed such a horrible crime. But I wouldn't be the last.

Some were there for evaluation before trials. Some, like me, were there because the system wasn't sure what to do with us. Some were too bat-shit crazy to go to trial and too dangerous to let loose.

A ten-year-old joined us when I was twelve, but he was a hardened ten whose father had pimped him to other men since he was six. He'd stabbed one of the "clients" and his father during one of the transactions. The other kids called him TwoFer and gave him a lot of respect. I was simply scared shitless of him.

Cowboy was a school shooter. Yes, a school shooter in Alaska. He unloaded on a class in his middle school. From all we could figure, his reasoning was that it seemed an easy path to stardom.

Slice 'N' Dice was into retro. He talked like a *Miami Vice* rerun. He was in for dismembering neighbors' pets and stashing the parts in their houses to provide them with a macabre kind of Easter egg hunt. Just fourteen, he was in for eval so he could be squirreled somewhere before he started dismembering people.

We went to classes, school-type and therapy-type. We had individual therapy, group therapy, regulated study time, and monitored free time.

We did it all moving about in cubes of gray. The floors were gray, the walls were cinder block covered with layer upon layer of thick gray paint. Hard. Unrelenting. No paintings (sharp edges), no bright colors (can aggravate aggressiveness), high ceilings with recessed fluorescent lighting (patients can't reach glass bulbs) needed for dark winter days.

But in summer, the light poured in the vast, unbarred windows (bulletproof glass) and bounced off the shiny walls and floors like the sounds did, echoing and amplifying. I hated the summer; the noise was bad enough. The light *and* the noise pushed me to the edge.

And *all* the inhabitants were edgy, so we took a lot of pills. Pills were the Loon Platoon's version of baseball cards. Barter and protection cloaked in another person's spit.

We were in art therapy once when Slice 'N' Dice sidled up close to Cowboy, TwoFer, and me.

"Hey, player."

He leaned in close to Cowboy. "I have info you might want, bro."

We were all white, but reality wasn't Slice 'N' Dice's long suit.

"What'll it cost me?" Cowboy asked.

"Tongue your sleeping pill, and give it to me tomorrow."

"Ask for one of your own."

Slice peeked over his shoulder and down the stark, gray linoleum-floored halls. "Man, they write all that down and give it to the Feds."

"And the Feds do what with that information?" Cowboy asked.

Slice scratched his head. "You want to know what's up or not?"

"Hey," I said. "I'll give you mine. Cowboy needs his." I'd take my own pill. By tomorrow Slice 'N' Dice would have forgotten or decided the missing pill was part of a global conspiracy.

He crooked his finger, motioning us forward, looking around, probably checking for federal listening devices. "There was another shoot 'em up," Slice said.

Cowboy turned to stone.

"Yeah. In Boston. Or maybe Maine. You know, lower forty-eight, it's all alike."

I watched Cowboy's face, but there wasn't even a flicker.

"This player did it up proud," Slice said. "More than you. Then he ate the gun."

I swear I saw Cowboy shimmer and dim.

"Player's gonna be famous, man. You're gonna be an also-ran."

"Get out of his face, Slice," I said.

Slice 'N' Dice's eyes raked me from head to foot. His voice turned lethal. "Man, you gotta learn to get along." He pulled away then looked over his shoulder. "You got a dog? I might get outta here someday."

That afternoon, Cowboy brought a broken toothbrush into his shrink's office, placed it against his own jugular, and jammed it home. Right in front of the doctor. Cowboy wanted that newspaper ink, even if he had to die to get it. He did die. I guess you can't put a tourniquet on somebody's neck.

We were all put in lockdown for twenty-four hours except for our private sessions and one group session on our floor. Did Slice goad Cowboy into suicide? In my mind Cowboy was a dead man since the day he shot up his classroom.

So what was I? Why hadn't I thought about offing myself? Why didn't I think about killing anyone else?

On my twelfth birthday, I came into The Frown's office, sat down, and put my newly big feet on his desk in imitation.

The Frown called this a different stage of denial. First I denied "the incident" with shock, loss of speech, loss of memory. Now I denied with attitude. The I-don't-need-to-talk-about-what-didn't-happen-dude 'tude. The Frown couldn't get me back to cartoon coyotes or remembering the smell of gasoline on a hot day in July.

"What's that?" I asked.

"Present. To you from me."

"Cool," I said. He'd never given me a gift — birthday, Christmas, nothing. Why didn't I see the trap about to be sprung?

I tugged the ribbon and opened the box. A baseball

glove. The color of leaves when they first drop to the ground.

I stared into the box like it was a well of lost secrets. The soft brown leather looked as supple as my mother's summer-tanned skin.

"It was his birthday present, too," I said.

"I know."

When I looked up, The Frown was blurred. His feet off the desk. "I interviewed Bobby's parents over a year ago. Asked them why Bobby came to your house that day."

"He was showing off his glove."

"Were you mad at him?"

I nodded, looking back into the box.

"I wanted to ruin the glove." I pushed my fingers through my hair, tugging for the pain. I closed my eyes. "I don't think I even saw Bobby. I just saw that glove. If I could get rid of it, if he didn't have it, we would be even, sort of."

"Are you sure you didn't want to hurt Bobby?" the Frown asked.

And for the first time ever, I *was* sure. Somewhere deep

the thought had been gnawing and chewing me, digging at me with sharp teeth where I couldn't identify what it wanted.

"I just wanted Bobby to go home. I didn't want him to hear the argument. I didn't want to hear it either. Everything Bobby had was good and my life was all in pieces. And he had that glove."

"And if you ruined the glove, he'd go home," The Frown said.

I nodded. "But I saw those flames . . . eat up Bobby's clothes and then his hair and his skin and he screamed and I screamed and then I knew. Nothing would be like the cartoons. And then zero. I couldn't hear it or see it and . . ."

I snatched the glove up out of the box and hurled it at the wall. "All this." I opened my arms. "All of *this*" — my voice broke and I fought back the tears that stung my eyes — "is Dad's fault. He left that gas out there. And a lighter. What kind of a father does that?" I leaned toward the desk. "I hate him for that. I was a little kid. None of this would have happened. Bobby would be alive and I would still be a kid, if he had . . ."

I couldn't be still, and jumped to my feet and paced. "And Aunt Jemma trying to take me away. I lost my mom, now she wants me to lose my dad and my home? My head hurt all the time. Just pound, pound, pound. Like somebody kicking me.

"And Mom. She went and died. I was nine years old. How could she do that to me?" I picked up the bowl of multicolored candies and flung them across the room. The plastic bowl made a decent thud against the door. "But . . . I — I am NOT a monster!"

"You're angry. You were carrying a lot of weight for someone that young. All the people that were supposed to protect you seemed to have let you down."

He had no idea how right he was. And there was also that secret I couldn't tell him.

"You," I shouted at The Frown, "need to know when to back off. You're going where you don't belong. Did you get your degree online or something?"

My shouting had alerted Orderly of the Day. He came through the door looking for action. I gave it to him. I launched at him and head-butted him square in the chest.

Instead I ended up on the floor and wasn't even rewarded with a satisfying "ummph" from OOTD. His chest was a brick wall and my head was a melon.

"I'm guessing you have another headache," The Frown said. He wasn't sarcastic. He was sad, like he expected all this. "I'm locking you in for a couple of days. You can have something for your head."

OOTD pointed me to the door without a word. I kicked the chair as I left.

We walked in silence until we reached the ward entrance. As he unlocked the doors, his deep voice was quiet, calm. "Every bit of that goes in your file. The judge reads it. Kicking the chair, everything. You don't want that."

"Fuck off."

"I'm not putting that on your record. You know why? You're not tough. You're broken."

Chapter 6
TOUCHSTONES

The pill for my headache put me down for a few hours. I woke up groggy and kept dozing in and out.

I saw some papers and crayons next to me. My homework must have been delivered when I was conked out. We didn't get pencils or pens when we were in lockdown. Nothing sharp.

I nodded back out. Half dreaming about how the teachers hated grading our homework from lockdown. Dozing. Dreaming about crayons. Dreaming about Mom.

"Goodness, Kip, are you angry at that picture?" Mom asked.

I was scribbling in hard, rough strokes, blotting out the picture of a moose in my coloring book.

She sat beside me at the table. "You broke the crayon."

She took my hand and rubbed it, easing the muscles, stretching each finger, rotating my wrist. "You're so much like your father. So tense."

She picked up a brown crayon and handed it to me, took a yellow one for herself. "Let's do this page together. Watch me for a minute." She gentled the crayon against the paper, smoothing the color into the shapes, staying inside the lines.

"Isn't that pretty?" Mom pointed to the page. "You try the tree trunk."

She showed me how to hold the crayon like she did. This time I didn't tear the page.

"Oh, that's beautiful. Now let's do the leaves," Mom said.

I put the crayon down. Trying so hard to go easy, to stay inside the lines, made me want to jump out of my skin.

Dad would have fussed about a job left unfinished, but Mom laughed. "Go. When you come back we can read."

I smiled at her as she helped me into my fur-ruffed hooded jacket.

Mom understood.

I learned to read earlier than most kids. As I sat in Mom's lap, she would read book after book, pointing to the words, showing me how they were alike and different. I don't know how or when it happened, but one day I was reading the words without her.

Dad read with me, too, but only one book. *The Runner.* It had been his when he was a kid. We read it a million times. After he'd read the last page, he'd close the cover, then run his fingers over the picture of the boy riding his horse, The Runner, with his dog, Shadow, trotting alongside him. Dad's fingers stroking the book reminded me of how he would sometimes touch my mother's cheek or hair, like he was praying for something.

"I'd never be without this book. . . . It's my touchstone."

Mom's mouth would go straight and a little hard, but then she'd sigh and relax. "It's where this all started, that's for certain."

I didn't ask what a touchstone was, but I knew there was something else between the covers of that book that I didn't understand.

Dad brought me *The Runner* when they moved me to the ward. Along with a picture of my mother. He thought those two things would be what I would want most, my treasured possessions.

I hadn't read the book since I was eight or nine. So while I was in lockdown I scrounged it up and read it. And I finally understood the pebble of resentment between my parents.

It's about a horse and a boy and a father that don't-can't-*won't* fit into regular society. They live on their own terms — not exactly wild, but free.

That's Dad for certain. And I was definitely wild, yet *not* free.

"Wild" or "free" really wasn't Mom at all. I think she

loved the beauty of Alaska, but the loneliness killed her just as surely as the cancer did.

And I think she let both of them do it.

For the next year I rode the anger train. I punched other members of the Loon Platoon. I tried to throw down on the orderlies, but they were bigger and tougher than I was. I fought walls and broke bones in my hands; I fought with my dad; The Frown; anyone, anything that crossed my path.

When I was in lockdown because of the fights, I read to pass the time. I checked out as many books as the roving library would let me, and the English teacher sent me some others. He put a note in with *War and Peace*.

> Kip,
> I didn't read this 'til I was a sophomore in college.
> But I think you can handle it.
>
> Mr. Cannon

I returned his kindness with sneering contempt.

Mr. C.,
I read it *last* year.
Mr. Kip

I fought using my mouth instead of my fist with Dad, too. We spent three of our weekly visits with Dad chatting and me glaring. When he tried to hug me before he left, I shrugged him off. The next time he came it was for a sit-down with The Frown.

I came in with Dad's copy of *The Runner.*

I plopped into my chair then tossed the book onto The Frown's desktop.

"You can have that back. I don't want it."

"Why?" Dad asked.

My first response was a disgusted sigh. Then: "Because it's yours."

The Frown broke the silence that followed. "Do you mean you don't want anything that belongs to your father, or that you feel it's not rightly yours but his?"

"Is there a difference?" I said.

"Kip, we're past crap like this. Don't manipulate," The Frown said.

"Fine. I want Dad to know I'm pissed."

"You made that clear when you wouldn't talk to me." Dad sounded sad, but he still had that hard bottom in his voice. Like a warm stream with a stony bed.

"I reread that book. And I remembered how Alaska was all about you. You had to live in the bush. You had to be 'free' like that guy in the book. You didn't care what Mom wanted. You didn't want a crowd around, but Mom was lonely. And you were all about work, work, work. Do this, do that. Work harder. It's not done until it's right."

I stood so I could, for once, be taller than Dad. "I was a kid, not your slave. And Mom wasn't either." Now I was shouting. "What happened to her, what happened to me — you were always right in the big middle."

Dad was on his feet and stepping into my face. "Sit down. Sit down and never, ever say anything like that to me again."

"Those aren't the rules here. You can't make the rules here." I stepped into him until we were chest-thumping.

Dad, red-faced and sweating, took a deep breath and looked to The Frown.

"Redirect," The Frown said.

Dad nodded, backed off, and sat down. He breathed in deep a few times, blowing the air out hard. Then he gripped the side of his chair so hard I could see the tendons standing out in his wrists, the scars from his burns white and ugly. Dad stared at the floor.

What the hell was going on?

"Sit down, Kip," The Frown said.

I sat.

"'Redirect' is a phrase from Anger Management classes. Your father took them, too."

Dad released his hands and rubbed them together. "Your mother always said that I flew off the handle at anything."

I perched on the edge of my chair. Now that this anger stuff finally wasn't all about *me,* I almost laughed. Instead, I picked up *The Runner* and banged it against the desk. WHAM! WHAM! WHAMWHAMWHAM! Then sidearmed it across the room.

I slammed out of the door into the grip of the Orderly of the Day.

The only place I could keep myself in check was in classes. Mom had homeschooled me, so I was used to doing things on my own.

Even though I was not quite thirteen, I had classes with the fourteen-year-olds. Most of them were finger-pointers and mouth-breathers, so it wasn't that big of a deal, but I got a lot of the teacher's time to discuss the books we read.

Close to Christmas he assigned "A Christmas Memory," by Capote. Then he showed the movie because he was pretty sure the mouth-breathers either didn't read it or didn't understand it. Hammer. Nail. Direct hit.

When the movie was over, the teacher asked for comments.

Zip. Zero.

Finally, a kid we called Toe Jam, because his foot odor announced his presence in any room, said, "If I got hold of some whiskey, I wouldn't pour it on a cake."

Scattered laughter.

The teacher put both palms on his desk and leaned forward. "What's the book about?"

A longtimer trying to ass-kiss his way into shaving off some of that time said, "Little kid and his whacko aunt making Christmas fruitcakes."

"Yes," the teacher said. "On the surface, but it's really about the innocence of childhood."

That lit my fuse with a blowtorch.

"Did you read the book or did you just read the words in order?" I asked.

"Excuse me?"

"You come in here every day with your sissy cappuccino and your starched khaki pants and you think we don't know that you wouldn't be here if anyone else, anywhere else, would hire you?"

"I think you —"

"Actually, you *don't* think. You just proved that."

"Take your seat, please —"

"Hold on. I'm not done. First, this isn't a book. It's a longish short story, and it's not a sweet little tale about the innocence of childhood. Get a grip.

"My mom taught me that when you read a book, you question it. Who is this kid and why is he there? Answer.

His mother doesn't want him. So she hands him over to his really poor, loony aunts. They don't want him either. So, innocence? Maybe not."

I looked around. The English teacher was glaring and the rest of the class looked like someone poked them in the eye with a sharp stick.

"The looniest of the aunts and the kid make cakes. Fruitcakes. That nobody wants. They waste the little money they have on something people are going to laugh at and throw away.

"And what's the *end* of the story? The dog dies. The aunt dies. Death and abandonment. Why does he write the book looking back when he's older? Because now he knows they were the town joke. That's his Christmas memory. Humiliation and pain."

I flipped the book on his desk. "There's more in a book than words, numbnuts."

That got me another stare-down session with The Frown and a two-day lock in, but I got to do my class work without morons around me. The Frown also told me that I got bonus points for excellent vocabulary. I don't know which word he thought a twelve-year-old shouldn't know: abandonment, humiliation, or numbnuts.

And when the State reviewed my case, there was no way this teen who couldn't begin to handle anger was going to be allowed to live among the peaceful and unsuspecting citizens of Alaska.

Chapter 7
CHANGING LANES

The last fight I remember having in the hospital was in the cafeteria. I was thirteen. A newbie came in. So full of himself it leaked out of his pores. The hip-rolling bad-boy walk, the I-don't-care slouch, and the don't-mess-with-me chin jut — this guy had it all. He slid his tray onto the table and started maiming the mystery meat with his plastic spork.

"Hey, losers. Good news. I'm here to run the place now. We'll get together and see who takes what drugs and I'll decide when you tongue your pills and give 'em to me."

He looked older and tougher than the group of us, but I had seen too many of his kind come and go and I had been in a bad mood for two years now.

"Sing that song at another table," I said.

"Think about who you're mouthin' off to, little man. I set my sister's cat on fire and made her watch. You think I can't make you give me a few pills?"

Six boys sat there and I'm not sure any one of them were breathing. Finally, Klepto, a kid that couldn't seem to stop stealing cars, two of which had been state troopers' vehicles, pointed at me and said, "Dude, this guy set fire to a kid when he was like in first grade or something."

I was done. I put down my milk and picked up my tray. The newbie looked across the table and I swear he smiled like he won the lottery.

"Serious? You torched a kid? What'd that feel like? Was it the sweetest thing ever?"

I don't think I knew I had come across the table at him until I had him on the ground. He probably had twenty pounds on me, but I had rage. It took two orderlies to drag me off.

"Your eye is looking better," The Frown said. "The other guy looks much worse."

"It's not funny." I said. I wasn't angry anymore. Just tired.

"What makes you feel so bad about it?"

I slumped down but locked in on The Frown. "That kid, the one who torched that cat? He wanted to know how it felt. Burning a person."

"I heard."

"So how's that make him different from you? From the lawyers, the judge, or even my dad? They all want to know how I felt."

"Kip. You know the difference."

"That's what I'm trying to tell you. I'm losing my way here." I stood up and headed for the door.

Antidepressants appeared on my med charts that night. I had just swerved from anger to depression with no turn signal and my tires screeching. First it was just not giving a shit, not showering or washing my hair. Then black moods, inability to sleep, or sleeping too much, lack of appetite, listlessness, and finally finding myself crying for no good reason.

"You're getting institutionalized. I don't want that." The Frown leaned on his desk, kind of toward me, trying to get through my don't-give-a-shit haze. "You don't want that."

"Why not? I can stay here. Not hurt anybody else."

"You still have time to be a kid. Go to school. A real one. Meet normal people. Kip, you haven't even hit puberty yet. You have a life ahead of you."

I sagged down further in the chair and rolled my eyes. "Right. A life full of fluffy kittens in cute baskets, blue skies, and a perfect jump shot?"

"Probably not, but I'm getting a vision of a fairly normal life as a smart-ass," The Frown said.

I shrugged.

The Frown started tapping his pen.

"Don't ever play poker," I said. "You'll be in debt up to your butt."

The Frown frowned.

"You have something you want to say and you're looking for the angle," I said, parroting words I'd learned from The Frown himself.

"I'm that easy?"

"The only person I've known longer than you is my dad."

"He's the subject of this chat," The Frown said.

I sat up. "Dad? Is something wrong?"

"Your dad is fine. We're going to have a group session. You, me, him, and someone he wants you to meet."

This time The Frown watched me frown. Then all the ducks quit quacking and got in a row.

"Whoa, Dad's got a girlfriend. A serious one."

"He wants to discuss . . ."

"Don't shimmy-shammy with me. Is he coming to tell me he's getting married?"

More tapping.

I started sorting the candies. "You're not even going to ask me how I'd feel about that?"

The Frown laughed. "If I did it would be admitting something."

I stopped sorting and tossed a red candy at him. "Has she been to see you yet? Did she ask if I'm going to set the house on fire while they're sleeping?"

"You know I can't tell her anything about you. Not without your consent. And I haven't met her."

"If she exists, you mean."

"Correct."

"I'll say this much. I don't care if she hates my guts and I hate hers."

And then my eyes welled up. Couldn't control it. "If she's good to Dad, well . . . you know, he's always been here. He keeps coming back. Dad deserves whatever little bit of good he can grab, you know?"

"Are you kissing my ass trying to get extra dessert or something?"

"Oh, yeah, that pudding is worth an ass-kissing. In fact, they probably taste a lot alike."

"You're a gross little fart. Go away and come back tomorrow."

Her name was Carrie, and she didn't seem nervous. Dad was nervous enough for everyone in the room and a small village in Taiwan, and he never let go of her hand. We made some chit and some chat, then Carrie said, "Can I be blunt with you, Kip?"

"Go for it," I said.

"Kip, I've been seeing your father for a while. He told me about you when he thought our situation was looking serious. I'll tell you now that the fact that this man is your father says good things for you. But I won't make a judgment call about a child based on what his parent has to say. You get that, don't you?"

I nodded.

"I'll also tell you that if it came to a choice between us, you father would choose you without hesitation. That's also a mark in your favor."

Carrie turned then and smiled at Dad. And when he smiled at her I knew something. Dad never relaxed or lit up from inside when Mom smiled at him. They were stretched tight and they darkened in each other's presence.

But there was something else I could see in Dad's smile. Carrie had saved his life.

"I'm going to ask you to allow me to have all the information I need before I get further into this," Carrie said. "If I marry your father, for all intentions, I take you into my life and I'll be part of your support system. When you come out of here, there's going to be a shit storm, and I want to be sure I believe in you as completely as I need to."

"You don't pull any punches, do you, Carrie?"

"Do you want me to?"

I turned to The Frown. "Do I just tell you she can see my files or do I sign something?"

"You and your father have to sign." He pushed some papers toward me. I signed without reading.

"What's this about a shit storm?" I asked.

Dad rubbed his hand over his mouth. "There have been a few . . . problems that your doctor and I thought would be better addressed when you were getting closer to release." Dad seemed uncomfortable.

"How bad? Just give me a clue. I can get details later."

Dad sighed. “Our name got leaked. The paper can’t print it, but people talk. Kip, you know how that goes. The whole, um, incident was in the papers. It even made national news, TV, the whole ball of wax. I’ve had to move once and my boss even had to ask me to leave my job because . . . Anyway, I don’t use our last name anymore. I use Mom’s maiden name. I don’t even live in Anchorage now.”

“Where are you living?”

“Talkeetna.”

“You drive all that way every week to see me?”

“It’s not bad.”

“In the winter. On ice?”

Dad shrugged. “It doesn’t matter, Kip.”

But it did matter. I’d been hurting him for all these years in ways I hadn’t even known. How much more was there?

Chapter 8
BITING THE GORILLA

I had my worst nightmare ever that night.

It was like those vampire movies. Long lines of people moving down the street with torches. They're screaming, "Bring him out. Let him feel what it's like." They swarm the house, the cabin, where I lived before. My dad goes to the door. I'm standing behind him. He goes out onto the porch and the whole screaming mob throws their torches at him. Dad goes up in flames as I watch, paralyzed because I see that the flaming things weren't torches. They're baseball gloves. Gloves of fire.

"Kip, hey, kiddo, wake up."

I jolted out of sleep to see one of the Ward Nazis leaning over me.

"You're okay. Settle down. Kiddo, you must have really bit the gorilla."

I was dripping sweat, my head was pounding and . . .

"What?"

"Bit the gorilla. Had a bad nightmare. You were screaming so loud it sounded like somebody bit a gorilla in here."

"It was more like the gorilla bit me."

She kind of squatted so she could look me in the eyes. "You okay? Want me to call the doc?"

"Nah, I think I can handle it."

"I can give you something to calm you down. You might not realize it, but you're twitching like a fly-bit horse."

I almost smiled at that one. "You think these things up to use when we go whacked-out on you? Bit the gorilla? Fly-bit horse?" I pointed my index finger at her. "I think you need to talk to Doc about this biting fixation."

"Don't give me your fifty-cent psychology. Do you

want serious pharmaceuticals to get back to sleep or do you want me to whip your skinny butt at chess?"

"Can I have hot chocolate?"

"Sure."

"I gotta warn you, I'm the best chess player on the ward."

"Honey, most of the people on this ward call the rook a horse and then bite its head off."

"And there you go again with the biting fixation." I couldn't play chess for shit. But I'd rather lose all night long than sleep and take another chance at that dream.

"Hey, um, I don't know your name," I said. "I'm usually asleep when you're on duty."

"You don't call me Ward Nazi like you do all the other ward nurses?"

Busted.

She laughed out loud. "That's okay, kiddo, it's the nurses that started calling you guys the Loon Platoon."

She must have noted my expression. "Hey, kid, even in a place like this, what goes around comes around."

That's pretty much what I was afraid of.

"I hear Belinda taught you to play chess," The Frown said.

"I knew how to play already."

"Not according to Belinda."

I grinned. "She might be right after all."

"A nightmare that bad — I think we need to talk about it."

"I'd rather talk about the shit storm Carrie mentioned. I want to know why Dad had to change his name."

"I figured as much," The Frown said. He dropped a thick folder on the desk and slid it toward me. "I have some videos too. News clips and a documentary about children killing children. They couldn't use your name, but it leads with your case. The Clarkes are interviewed. Your cabin is shown." He pulled three videos out of a drawer and stacked them on the desk.

"I've got paperwork to do. I suggest you read first. Ask me anything you want. Say anything you like. You're free to vent. When you're through reading we can watch the videos together. Then we'll talk. I've blocked the whole afternoon for you."

"A whole afternoon? You think I'm at a big turning point?"

"You turn often enough, you end up straight ahead again. Let's just say it's gonna be a rough day."

"Then I'm heading for the couch." I gathered up the file and stretched out on the couch, wadding a pillow under my neck.

My name was never printed. But my home was pictured as the scene of the crime. The first reports were unclear. Two juveniles were involved and both were hospitalized. One for burns. As soon as it became clear that one juvenile was responsible for the fatal burning of the other, "the crime" became "the heinous crime."

I read ranting letters to the editor about criminals hiding from prosecution behind their age, furious letters about protecting the community from its "bad seeds." One woman's letter quoted the Bible's teaching that seven was the age of reason and so the nine-year-old devil child needed to go to hell and learn what burning was all about.

"Is seven really the age of reason?" I asked.

"You reading those letters to the editor?"

I nodded.

"That's fear talking. Something happened that people don't understand. Something that was out of anyone's control. So the easiest thing is to throw you away. Put you out of sight so you won't scare them anymore. They pick the easy side to be on — the side of the most obvious victim."

"What do you mean? Bobby was the only victim."

The Frown took off his glasses and rubbed the little red marks on each side of the bridge of his nose. He replaced his glasses and adjusted them carefully before he looked at me. "We got victims here to stack up. Bobby is the dead one."

I couldn't think of anything to say.

"The Clarkes are victims, but they don't have to feel guilt like you do."

"I'm a victim?"

"You and your dad. Absolutely. Your lives are changed

in every way. Will be affected every day. You'll never shed the burden of guilt. Your dad feels the guilt of leaving you out there with the gas and the lighter. And now that you're learning all this . . ." — he gestured toward the file — " 'stuff,' shame's going to ride your shoulder like a vulture on a branch."

"Devil child," I said, looking back at the clipping.

"That's what your neighbors believe."

I had spent all my time here dealing with my guilt, my issues. My circle only broadened to include Dad, Bobby, and Mom, but I was still the center. How had I never considered what other people thought of what I'd done? I knew what the Loon Platoon thought.

"How did the rest of the world disappear for me? Why didn't it occur to me that so many people would . . ." I didn't know how to finish. I dropped the article back into the pile.

"That's what I meant about being institutionalized. You were young, just out of a coma. And I didn't want you to stress about the outside world yet. Now, it's time to consider the ramifications."

I gave a half nod and picked up another clipping. It dealt with the hospitalization of the "juvenile offender," his inability to stand trial, and the probability of a plea agreement.

The next page stunned me. A picture of the blackened, smoking remains of our cabin.

I held up the picture.

The Frown nodded. "Your dad was here in Anchorage with you. You lost everything except for a few clothes he had with him and the framed picture of your mother he brought down here for you. All the photographs of you as a child, of your mom, all of it is gone."

He took the picture from me and put it back in the folder.

"You can't go home again, Kip."

I nodded, numb.

"That's something your father wants me to speak with you about."

I looked up, still unable to speak.

"He and Carrie want to move to the lower forty-eight

when you leave here, and he wants you to consider changing your name."

"Sure. He said he uses Mom's name. That's fine."

"A little more than that. Kip is a noticeable name. Kip from Alaska. Somebody, somewhere, sometime is going to put things together."

"Change my first name, too?"

"I know it's a lot."

"Let's see — no mother, house, home, past, last name, first name? I won't know who I am."

"It might feel that way at first."

It would feel like erasing myself. Well, maybe Kip McFarland shouldn't be around anymore. Bobby Clarke wasn't. Could I shed Kip's guilt along with his name?

I looked down at the photo of the burned cabin again. Dad had built the cabin himself.

"I'll do whatever Dad wants."

Chapter 9
LEARNING TO WADE

As the day came nearer for my release, as I talked with lawyers and another shrink and a judge and then waited for all of the eggs to be put into my basket, I got scared.

"Why can't I stay here? Carrie and Dad can get married and live happily ever after. I know how to live here. How am I supposed to go to school? How do I make friends? The opening line here is 'What are you in for?' "

"You're scared. That's normal. You're whining. That's not like you."

"I'm not whining."

"See, you're doing it again."

I reached for the candy bowl. The Frown snatched it away.

"Give me a break, Kip. You're past that behavior. If you don't know what to do, then make a plan. I'll help you start. What's your new name?"

"Pissant."

"It fits, but it won't look good on the teacher's roll. Try again."

That no-nonsense tone from The Frown. I sighed and drummed my fingers on the arms of the chair.

After a few minutes my eye lit on the back of one of The Frown's sailing mags.

"Wade."

The Frown said "Wade" like he was testing it. "Good. Got a reason or do you just like the sound?"

I pointed to the mag. A young man was wading out to a sailboat pulled close to a beach. "When you wade, you're kind of bogged down. You can't walk, or run; you're not swimming; you're kind of fighting the water all the time."

"But you're still moving forward when you wade."

"Optimists can be such downers," I said.

The Frown stood up and put out his hand. "Okay, now, let's try this. 'Hello, Wade, I'm Don Schofield.' "

Well, now The Frown and I both had new names.

"Glad to meet you, Dr. Schofield." We shook hands.

"And I'm kicking your ass out of here in three weeks." He sat back down.

"That's too soon."

"Tough. I'm tired of you. You're too sane to be interesting now."

"Three weeks?"

"You'll be ready. Trust me," Dr. Schofield said. He turned his chair in a complete circle then stopped. "There's something I want you to do. When you get some computer time in the dayroom, I want you to look up a phrase. It's 'feeding the hungry ghost.' See what it says. Think about it. Make sure you don't do it."

Later I Googled the phrase, which sent me to a site that had the Buddhist Wheel of Life. Wheel Twelve:

Hungry Ghosts

Characterized by – Greed; Insatiable cravings; Addictions. "I want this. I need this. I have to have this."

This is the realm of intense craving. The Hungry Ghosts are shown with enormous stomachs and tiny necks – they want to eat, but cannot swallow; when they try to drink, the liquid turns to fire, intensifying their thirst. The torture of the hungry ghost is not so much the frustration of not being able to get what he wants; rather, it is his clinging to those things he mistakenly thinks will bring satisfaction and relief.

So, I'm going out into the world and The Frown is leaving me with a Zen riddle for advice?

Great.

For three weeks, I practiced being a real person.

"This is how it works. Even though high school is full of elitists, boneheads, and jerks, they'll be a walk in the park compared to the Loon Platoon."

"I've never walked in a park," I said.

"It's like walking in the woods without the bears." The Frown looked me over. "I'd consider cutting your hair. But wait until you move and get a look at the people in your town. This is Alaska. I don't have a clue what young people in the real world do to their heads."

"This is so encouraging," I said.

"Whatever you wear the first day of school will be wrong. Trust me on this."

"Tell me again what good this is doing me?"

"If you depend on television for fashion, it's either ahead of the times or way behind. Wear jeans and a casual shirt of some kind. Then the best way to make a friend or get someone to like you is to ask him for help. You know, throw up your hands and say, 'Obviously I need help with this. We don't know how to dress out in the boonies.' "

"That works?"

"Oh, hell, yes. Makes a person feel good. Superior, even. Taking someone under their wing. Totally effective. But do it with a sense of humor — don't be whiney or needy."

"Were you popular in high school?"

"I was a nerd."

"So, you learned all this from books."

"Nope, learned it from watching the popular kids. I was skinny and wore thick glasses and was in the band. You, though, are good-looking, have a long, lanky, athletic build, and when you're not whining or swinging your fists, there's something resembling wit. You can make this work."

"I *am* really good-looking, aren't I?" I dripped with sarcasm, but I wondered if he was shining me or . . . I didn't know.

"And so humble. Now, first day. Everyone will stare at the new kid."

"In his totally wrong clothes."

"Right. Someone might say something crappy about you or your clothes. He'll be a lowlife. It's important that you ignore him or make a joke."

"So I don't get expelled for fighting on my first day," I said.

"That and because giving pond scum attention is not cool."

"Oh. Cool."

"You'll be late to almost every class because you won't

know how to get there. You'll have to stand at the front to get signed onto the teacher's roll."

"More staring."

"It'll be like when the gorilla takes a dump at the zoo. Everybody has to come look."

"I'll be gorilla shit for the day?"

The Frown laughed. "Indeed you will. Be ready."

"And people do this to their children?"

"On purpose," The Frown said.

"And the State thinks *I'm* crazy."

"Now, somebody asks where you're from. How do you answer the question?"

"Locked up with the other rabid animals?"

The Frown didn't think I was funny.

"Fine, I say 'Alaska.' If that isn't enough I tell them I lived in the bush. If they still seem to want more details, I start in on Alaska stuff, how I was homeschooled, and then stuff about moose and bears and snow and no igloos. Pull attention away from details about me that they can prove or disprove."

"Good. You could work for the CIA."

"Yeah, I hear they're looking for assassins." There was a long silence.

"Now that's feeding your hungry ghosts," Doc said.

I slumped back in the chair and scrubbed my face with my hands. "I'm not sure I got all that."

"I'm not trying to turn you into a Buddhist, but the idea runs along with Western therapy for addiction. Any addiction is your hungry ghost. Booze, food, anorexia, drugs, and emotional cravings. What's your hungry ghost, Wade?"

"Wade doesn't have any ghosts. He's brand-new."

"Bull. He's carrying Kip's baggage. What's Kip's ghost? What's he crying out for?"

"That's what I don't get," I said.

"Guilt," Doc said. "But truth is the only thing that will shut up the ghost and give you peace."

The Frown looked like he was waiting for something from me. I still didn't get it.

"What do you want, Kip?"

I thought a long minute. "To be normal. To be just like

everyone else. To not have burned a kid to death. To forget it ever happened and live my life."

"Is that possible?" Doc asked.

"I'm going to try like hell," I said.

The plan was to release me at one minute past midnight. Even though court records are sealed, information gets around. The Anchorage papers had already run a story that the child murderer was being released under a new identity. Carrie and Dad picked me up. Doc Schofield and Belinda were there to say good-bye.

Belinda gave me a travel chess set. "Lord knows you need practice," she said. "And don't go biting any gorillas, you hear?"

I grinned at her. "Doc, the woman needs professional help about this biting thing."

"I would, but she scares me," he said.

Belinda lifted one eyebrow and gave him the evil eye. "At least the man is smart. He *should* be scared of me." She squeezed me in a long hug.

Dr. Schofield shook my hand. "Go, live, be happy. Doctor's orders."

Wade set a little boy on fire?

He killed a child.

When Wade was a child he murdered a child?

No, not Wade. I don't even know Wade. He's Kip.

Kip?

I don't know Kip.

But I don't know Wade either, do I?

He'd been in a . . . what exactly was it anyway? A hospital for the criminally insane?

They'd all lied to me from the beginning. Not only Wade, but his father, and Carrie. This "secret" was so hideous no one could know his name. Could know anything about him. About them.

What were their real names?

Were they afraid of him? Is he still dangerous? He harbored guilt and anger that raged inside him for years. What kind of damage does years of this do to a person that's already damaged?

Do you get to kill someone and say, "Oh, really sorry now," and everything is fine?

I closed the second book. I didn't want to read any more. I had already read too much.

I went downstairs to get some coffee.

Dad was at the kitchen table working on his sermon.

I sat. "Dad, talk to me about redemption. Is it possible for any sin?"

Dad's eyebrows rose. "Are we talking about you?"

I hadn't been, but his question made me pause. My silence must have been a positive answer for him.

"Redemption is often confused with forgiveness. To redeem yourself you must change, become stronger; sometimes you must make amends if you have caused harm to another. Forgiveness — well, I have my own views on forgiveness."

My eyes got cloudy and wet. "Have you forgiven me?"

My father put his hand on mine. "I refuse to forgive anyone because that implies that I'm superior — that I have a right to make a judgment. As if I haven't fallen to temptation or will never fall. What a load of horse manure."

"But . . ."

"What I know is that you ran into something you were too young to understand. What I know is that there's a history of this in my family. How could you know what you were dealing with? I can't forgive you. Do I forgive someone who falls down and is injured? No, I help them recover."

I breathed out. "Are you angry that I don't go to church anymore, Dad?"

"Now, that's about forgiveness. You haven't forgiven yourself. You think you aren't worthy to be in God's house."

I tensed. "No, I'm fine. I know what happened to me and made my peace with it."

"And that's why you hide out here at the beach. You sail, you go to class, you study. The only people I've seen you speak to are the new neighbors. People that don't know your past."

So, had I lied to them as much as they lied to me?

I started the conversation wondering about redemption for Wade. I ended wondering about forgiving myself.

Nothing is ever easy. There's never a straight road.

I made coffee. I would be reading for a while.

PART II
INDIANA

Chapter 10
THE "GO" PART

I was Wade Madison and had papers to prove it. Son of Jack and Carrie Madison. New residents of Whitestone, Indiana. I had a new backpack and a class schedule and the totally wrong clothes. Alaska is all about flannel. Indiana looked to be all about long-sleeved tees. I had the wrong shoes. At least I was prepared to be wrong.

I figured nothing new happens often in Whitestone, Indiana, because I got the total stare down when I got on the bus. It didn't help when some kid that looked all of ten stuck his foot in the aisle and I tripped over it. My first thought was to break his leg off at the knee and let him carry it in his backpack, but I kept it together while some of the bus riders laughed and others continued staring. I sat at the back, so they had to work to look.

By the time I found my locker, my totally wrong clothes and shoes had moved from the abstract to fact. "Do you think he's homeless?" was one of the nicer snippets of conversation I picked up in the halls. I couldn't get the combination lock to work until my fifth try, and I was red-faced and sweating when I stood like a dumb ass in the hall trying to figure out where the hell corridor C could be.

I finally blundered into my first class ten minutes late: English I. Kind of a combo of reading, writing, and whatever else the teacher finds to broaden the minds of freshmen.

I handed the teacher my form.

"Wow, Alaska. You're a long way from home."

I nodded. At least the teacher thought I had a home. A quick look at the class made the blush and the sweat return. Most of them stared at me like they thought I'd crawled out from under a bridge.

"What brings you here, Wade?" the teacher asked.

I had the Wade thing down now. And my story. "My stepmom got sick of the dark winters. Dad got a job here."

"I see you were homeschooled."

Was the sweat showing? Did I have huge pit rings on my shirt? Could the earth swallow me whole?

"We lived pretty far out, not in a town. Homeschooling is common in Alaska." Okay, that last part sounded way rehearsed. The Frown and I had practiced a little too much.

"Take a seat, Wade. You can choose the empty one." The teacher grinned like she was a stand-up comic. This was going to be a long day.

"Ms. Bales?"

"Yes, Justine?"

"Can we ask the new guy stuff about Alaska?"

"What do you say, Wade? I'll admit I'm interested, too."

I gave her the "I'm cool with that" chin jut.

"All right, class, Wade is open for questions. Introduce yourself before you ask him anything, please."

A boy with an enormous square head with hair so blond and short he looked bald spoke first. "So, dude, I'm Dave. Did you, like, live in an igloo?"

The teacher rolled her eyes.

Was I ever going to be able to sit down?

"No, we lived in cabins and regular houses, but no igloos. I noticed that here in the lower forty-eight there are lots of brick houses. There's not much brick in Alaska."

"Have you ever seen a polar bear? I'm Justine."

"No, I did see black bears and a few grizz." Flashes of TwoFer and his dead-eyed stare, or Cowboy and that toothbrush swept through my mind, and I knew I'd seen way scarier things than polar bears during my four years on the ward.

"What about penguins?"

"Introduction, please?" Ms. Bales said.

"Brandon."

I shook my head. "Penguins, South Pole. Alaska, North Pole."

A couple of people laughed. The guy named Dave coughed the words "dumb ass" behind his hand, and a really good-looking girl said "du-uh." Then she curiously blew a kiss at the knucklehead.

The stares had turned to interest in the subject, and I didn't feel so troll-like now. I wondered if I was still red-faced.

"How cold does it get? I'm Amber."

"In the interior it's not unusual to have a few days of fifty and sixty below."

"No way!"

"Thank you, Anthony," said Ms. Bales. "But, Wade, can a person breathe air that cold?"

I hadn't lived in the interior since I was nearly ten, but I could remember Mom wrapping a wool scarf around my nose and mouth before taking me out in the cold. I was swamped with longing for the old cabin. For the moose that would munch on the willow branch outside my window. For my mom. Right now, even for the safety of the doc's office.

"Hmm, right, that kind of cold can damage your lung tissue. You have to have something over your nose and mouth and breathe through it to warm the air first. Or better, stay inside. When it's that cold, most Alaskans are smart enough to stay where it's warm."

"I'd like to know about how long it stays dark, and then we need to get on with our lesson," Ms. Bales said.

"Depends on what part of Alaska. Farther north, the bigger the differences. In the interior in the dead of winter you've got about three or four hours of daylight. Summer, you've got about two or three hours of dark, and that isn't real dark kind of dark."

"Midnight hoops! Sweet," Dave said.

I nodded, even though the Loon Platoon hadn't played a lot of midnight hoops.

Ms. Bales set the class up with a reading assignment and called me to her desk to show me a list of things they had read that semester. As I scanned the list I saw that I was light-years ahead of this group.

"I'm good here. Homeschooling gives you lots of reading time." I pointed at one title. "That's the only one I haven't read."

"Since you've read the Poe stories the class is working

on now, why don't you read *The Light in the Forest* independently? I'll give you a written assignment when you're done so I can assess your writing skills."

She dug in a cabinet and handed me a worn paperback, and I dogged back to my desk. Ten minutes into my first class, school had been mood-swingy, but with nobody to hand me lithium in a little paper cup. When I stood waiting for the bus, it seemed impossible that I could walk into a place with so many normal people. Those stares and trips and comments in the hall somehow seemed more brutal than the ward. But except for that flash of homesickness, the rest had gone pretty much like Doc had said.

After I escaped into *The Light in the Forest* for the two-hour block, the bell rang and I checked my list to see where I was headed next. The square-headed kid stopped at my desk. "Lemme see?" He pointed to my schedule card. When I handed it to him, he fanned it and said, "Who'd you kill, man? They did you wrong."

My skin crawled and my heart stuttered. Then I realized it had to be just an expression.

"Must be because you were homeschooled and transferred from Siberia or wherever, but they put you with the brain-dead."

"Is the room in this hall or where?"

"Come on, I'll walk you over. That way I can miss part of speech. I hate that class." He handed me back the schedule and gestured for me to accompany him. I scrabbled for my backpack and tried to keep up.

"I'm not from Siberia. I'm from Alaska," I said.

"Yeah, yeah, cool. Whatever. Listen, here's the deal. Most of us take Indiana history in, like, eighth grade and it's easy-peasy, but you have to pass it or they, like, throw you out of the state or something, so if you're a dumb shit or if you have to, like, unzip to count to twenty-one, you might have to take it again as a freshman, so I'm telling you this for free. There's going to be some real night crawlers in your class. And those leeches love to welcome newcomers. If I was wearing those weird-looking shoes, I'd do my time and not make any close, personal friends. But if you have a drug habit, it's the place to connect."

He took a breath. Again, my heart hiccuped.

"So?" he asked me.

"So? I asked. "What?"

"So, are you a druggie?"

Yes, I'm pharmaceutically fueled, but prescription only, I felt like saying.

"Nope, but I was wondering something?"

"What's that?"

"Why in the world *you* wouldn't like your speech class."

Square-headed Dave gave a laugh that sounded more like a truck backfiring. "It's because the teacher keeps letting those *other* people talk." He pointed me to my door. "I don't even want to get too close to that room. Could hurt my cool quotient."

One of the "night crawlers" walked past us on his way into the class. "You rob a homeless dude for those shoes, loser?"

I glanced at Dave. Then to the night crawler: "Family heirloom. Grandma loved these shoes."

Chapter 11
UGLY PUP AT THE POUND

The things I noticed most about the Indiana history class was that there was a lot of eyeliner and tattoos. The kicker was that the eyeliner was on the guys and most of the visible tats were on the girls. The guys were like cartoon people: dog collars on wrists and necks, leather vests, and eyeliner. Black, neon, sparkly. Did a whole cult of Maybelline-inspired XY chromosomes get together and flunk Indiana history? Did the flunking of history produce this behavior? Was there tangerine eyeliner in my future?

But something about this class felt familiar. It was quiet. Not because everyone in class was hard at work, but because there was a disconnect. Most of my fellow students doodled idly, slept, or stared vacantly. They were appliances left unplugged. I got my book and read Indiana history. I'd wear eyeliner and get a tat before I'd check out of life.

When the bell rang, I walked out looking over my list for the next class when it was snatched out of my hand.

My old reaction was to swing a fist first and ask questions never, but I ground my teeth and looked to see who had grabbed my schedule.

"Here you go, Kemo Sabe." Four-cornered Dave.

I unclenched and took a calming breath.

"I told the speech teacher I was mentoring a new student." He handed the class schedule back. "Don't give me that look. I'm on student council. She totally bought it. And face it — you're like the puppy at the pound that's so ugly it's almost cute, ya know? If I don't watch out for you, the big dogs will chew you up by noon. Don't thank me now. Cash will be appropriate at a later time."

"I'm supposed to pay you for calling me an ugly dog?"

"Now, that's putting a harsh on it."

He gave that one-fingered let's go motion and took off. I shouldered my pack and followed, since I was the ugly puppy at the pound.

"Algebra. Not bonehead math. That homeschooling must work. And you've got the teacher everybody wants. Not much homework. I'll take you in and the rabble will see you're under my protection. You'll be fine."

He sailed in the door. "Hey, Mr. Schultz. I have the new kid for ya. From Siberia, no less."

"Alaska," I said.

"Same thing," Dave said. "He can tell you great stories about snow and stuff."

"Thank you, Dave. Have you adopted this young man or is there a test you'd like to be late for?"

"I *would* like a late pass, Mr. S. I'm mentoring Wade here as part of the student council program and . . ."

"I seriously doubt that, Dave, but to get rid of you, I'll do anything short of payment. Well, I might resort to payment." He handed Dave a pass. "Go, and go quickly, before I lose all hope for your generation's future."

Dave flapped off a half-assed salute and sauntered out. Schultz made a shooing motion. "Faster, lout, faster."

Mr. S. was youngish, maybe my dad's age, and the geezer talk didn't seem to fit. It seemed almost like a rehearsed thing between them.

I handed my form to Schultz. He signed it, handed me a book. "So, where did you meet my son?"

"Square-headed — ummm, Dave is your *son*?"

"Yes. His blockhead is a chip off my own. I see you didn't know that."

"He didn't mention it, sir."

"Please forget it immediately. The child is demented. Take a seat, please, and tell us a bit about Alaska."

And I went through the same questions: polar bears, penguins, igloos, the cold, and the dark. But this time I was more answering questions than feeling like I was reciting lines from a play Doc and I had written.

In fact, I finally got comfortable enough to test Doc's throw-yourself-on-their-mercy theory.

"You guys are gonna have to help me out a little. Living out in the boonies, we didn't care how we dressed. Anything that kept us warm was fine. Somebody has to show me what works here. Flannel and duck shoes don't look like they're 'in' in Indiana."

The absolutely cutest girl in the room said, "Hey, I can shop like a Harvard grad. I'll help."

Doc was a genius.

Mr. Schultz said, "My son is most adept in spending someone else's money. He's also supposed to do chores for his mother this weekend, so I'm quite certain he would find his assistance to your cause crucial at that time."

I don't know why this guy talked the way he did, but I kind of liked it. I pictured him in a class full of guys from the Loon Platoon. I'd love to overhear a convo between Slice 'N' Dice and Mr. Schultz.

Schultz used his strange vocabulary and phrasing with a sense of humor, and he clearly thought we were intelligent enough to understand him. The class returned the respect. I felt a sense of déjà vu, like when I slid into the chair in Doc's office and we slipped into our routine.

The day swung back to bipolar when I hit the gym. I had heard the term "corn-fed" about the Midwest population before, but how much corn had they fed them? These guys standing around in shorts had biceps and quads that were bigger than my head.

I was new and skinny. Call me *target*.

I had bought a pair of shorts and a T-shirt, but I hadn't bought a pair of sneakers yet. The right kind of athletic shoe was critical, Doc had told me, and I had to check what the locals wore before I bought a pair. So, for my first class I played in my duck shoes.

The game was Scramble. A kinder, gentler dodgeball. Rule: ball hits below the knee. But there's an acre of hurt between knee and toe. And I was about to be schooled.

Bam! "Hey, new kid, did that hurt?"

Zing, thwamp! "Alaska, you better go home and put some snow on that."

Thwack! "Didn't they have a gym at that home school?"

Thud! "Dude, seriously, those stupid shoes are slowing you down. This isn't even fun anymore."

And the agony didn't stop on the gym floor. I limped my way to the showers only to come out to find my towel missing. I slicked off most of the water, trying to take it in stride, and then walked to the bench to find my clothes gone, too. The thumping started in my head hard and loud, but I shook if off, slicking the anger away as I had the water drops.

The few guys still hanging around for the show shrugged and high-fived as they left. I sat, naked as a plucked chicken, shivering and goose-pimpled as the next class filed in.

"Could someone ask the coach to come here?"

"Look, kid, I'll have every one of those little jerks in this office, and in two minutes I'll have your clothes back and their butts in detention."

I didn't know how this worked in high school, but on the ward that could have gotten me killed. I sat in the coach's office in a cast-off pair of football sweats and my bare feet.

"I'm seriously asking you not to do that."

"It's my job to do that."

"I get that, I do. But it's your job to help your students. I'm your student and I'm asking for your help."

"You're letting these boys off scot-free. Doesn't that rev your motor, son?"

I looked down at my bare feet. Rev my motor? My motor was in overdrive, but my ghost was hungry and I was going to feed it.

"Can you let me handle this? Please?"

The coach slammed his palms down on the desk. "You want to be a knucklehead? Go ahead."

"I need to go to the rest of my classes. These sweats you loaned me are fine." They were a few sizes beyond huge, and the sleeves slid over my hand, the legs bunched in folds, and the crotch hung to my knees.

"But I need something on my feet." I pointed to a pair of rubber boots in the corner. "If you have a pair of socks somewhere I could wear those."

"My boots? You'll walk out in those hallways in sweats and boots twenty sizes too big for you?"

I nodded.

"Son, you're a whole new kind of fish." He disappeared for a minute or two and returned with a pair of thick socks. He dropped them in my lap then placed the boots next to my chair.

I was majorly late to computer class. A couple of the gym bullies were there. The teacher did a double take at my attire but said nothing. Nobody said a word. No Alaska questions here.

When class was over, I clunked down the hall in the too-big boots, and a hole opened around me as I walked. I hiked my shoulders back and tried to put a strut on. The oversized boots turned strut to spastic, but I kept my head up and gave anyone that dared make eye contact a smile and a nod like this was part of the established dress code.

I got to earth science and the absolutely cutest girl in the room (from algebra) cruised in behind me.

"Oh. My. God." She circled me. "It's impossible. You got . . . even worse." She pulled my admission form from my fingers and dropped it on the teacher's desk. "Be kind, Ms. Strohm, and let him sit by me. It's looking like he's had a hard day."

The teacher signed the form. My outfit didn't seem to faze her. "Be sure to get a book from the back."

"*Who* did *what* to you?" Absolutely Cutest asked as she got my book and herded me toward a desk. "Somebody took your shoes?"

I sat without reply.

"And your clothes?"

I gestured, palms up.

"Did someone, like, tie you up or . . . Oh. My. God. You had gym, didn't you?"

"Don't worry about it. If your eyes fall out of your head, I don't know how to put them back in," I said. "They could end up all crossed or upside down or something."

She turned around in her desk. Then back again. "The shoes . . . not really a loss. Even if it was a mean trick." She smiled.

Mood on the upswing.

Chapter 12
HUNK O' LOVE

I caught the bus and endured the ride home. I made like a harbor seal and closed out the sounds around me as I reviewed the ups and downs of the day. Stares tinged with revulsion, down. Walking among people that weren't obvious psychopaths, up. Tripping on bus, down. Feeling lost, stupid, and alien, down. Overhearing hostile comments, way down. Watching hostile stares become looks of interest, up. Having an odd but seemingly decent guy make himself my guide dog, up. Some decent teachers, up. No orderlies accompanying me through doors that are locked at each corridor, way up. Being a target in Scramble, down. Sitting naked on bench, down. Wearing coach's sweats and boots, so down it's hard to find up. Absolutely Cutest's big wide smile, so up I can't remember down. And that was just the first day. The ward was never like this.

By the time Carrie got home from her job, I had washed and dried the sweats and socks and was dressed in my own clothes. I realized I had to go to school in a pair of moccasins tomorrow, when the phone rang.

"Hey, Siberia. Get your bad self ready. My mom is picking you up in thirty and taking us to the mall. She says if your mom wants to come to supervise the cash flow, it's cool, and she'd like to meet her. We're meeting Lindsey there."

"Is this Dave?"

"I heard you can't be trusted to choose new footwear."

"Do you take in all the strays that appear at your school?"

He sighed. "Lindsey called me."

"Who's Lindsey?"

"Big smile, big eyes, totally good-looking, in your algebra and earth science classes?"

"Oh, her." Absolutely Cutest. Wow.

"Yeah, her. She called and told me about the boots and the sweats. I told Dad. He called Coach Tulling. Coach told Dad that you wouldn't narc and wouldn't let him do anything to find out who took your stuff. Dad told Mom. Mom said for me to call. I told her about Lindsey. Do I have to go through the whole thing? Come on, Mom's buying slices at the mall."

"Hang on."

By eight we were in the mall. Carrie was in a Starbucks with Mrs. Schultz, and I was scarfing pizza with Dave and Absolutely Cutest. I had a few bags with long-sleeved tees, a couple new pairs of jeans that didn't look so "frontiersy," a hoodie, and the athletic shoe of choice that was in my price range.

Three boys that looked remarkably similar smiled, waved, and started in our direction.

"What's up, Schultz? Lindsey? Hey." The last was

directed to me. One scooted into the booth and the other two grabbed chairs, turned them backward, and straddled them.

"Wade, these are the three B's in a pod." One of the B's rolled his eyes. The other two didn't react at all.

The eye roller said, "I'm Brett, first cousin, a month older than these two and way better lookin'."

One of the guys hanging over the chairs made a little chin jut and said, "Brandon. I'm in language arts with you."

"Brendan," said the other.

"Brandon and Brendan are twins," Lindsey said.

"The B's' parents own a nursery and landscape business, so they practically grew up in the same playpen. If you find one, the other two will be close," Dave said. "Don't bother learning their names. Just yell "B!" and one of them will answer. And oh, yeah, they, like, invented religion, so don't swear around them. If one of 'em hears a cussword he'll faint, and the others will see and go down like dominoes."

The one in the booth (Brett?) pointed a finger at Dave

and squinted one eye. “The fact that Schultz here is still alive and walking the earth is proof of a merciful God.”

One of the B’s straddling the chair said, “I saw you in the hall today. The whole school knows who took your clothes, dude, and you walked those halls and made ’em yours. Good move.”

“The whole school knows?”

“It’s a little town and we got nothing to do but talk. You’re new and were pretty interesting today,” Dave said.

Great. I wanted to fly under the radar, blend in, lie low. And now I was the talk of the town.

“Look, I just didn’t want to make waves. No real harm done.”

“Are you like Gandhi or something? Wasn’t he the guy that wouldn’t squash a bug and wore a diaper?” This from Dave.

“Yeah, that’s me.” *The Anger King of the Loon Platoon, the kid who burned another kid being compared to the guy who wouldn’t step on an ant.* I shrugged. “Really, it’s wasn’t a big deal. Lindsey said the shoes needed to go anyway.”

"Definitely. You're cute, but not cute enough to overcome those shoes."

Dave cleared his throat. "Shiny, smiley faces everyone, moms at three o'clock and closing fast," he said.

After we all said our good-byes, Carrie and I headed for the car.

"Now that it's pretty much over, how was your first day?" she asked.

I thought a minute. "It really wasn't bad. A couple of people were lousy to me and a couple more were really great. I think I can make this work."

"I get paid next week; you'll need more shirts."

"Thanks, Carrie."

"I noticed that the cute girl was noticing you noticing her."

"Carrie . . ." It was a warning.

"Just stating facts."

"Your facts are wrong. She might be noticing me, but I'm not so much noticing her." I rubbed my nose with the back of my hand. "Okay, I noticed she was cute."

Carrie smiled at me.

"Carrie, can I ask you something weird?"

"Hmmmm, I hope fourteen weird isn't out of my league."

"It's just, I grew up in kind of a strange environment."

"Understatement," Carrie said.

"Somebody today — well, the cute girl, said *I* was cute. And I don't have a clue. Doc told me I was good-looking, but that's therapy stuff. To make you feel confident. But the girl? Is that the truth, or was she making fun of me?"

Carrie turned to look at me. "You know, it makes sense that you have two names. There's this 'you' that's far too grown-up, the one with the therapy mind-set and vocabulary, always examining his emotions." She sighed and smiled. "And then there's the 'you' that's so naive. Because you haven't lived in a real world at all. You're like a little bird that fell out of the nest."

She rapped the top of my head lightly with her knuckles and began walking again. "The answer is yes, Wade, you're cute. That girl was definitely not making fun of you. You're what I think girls refer to as a 'hottie.'

You look like your dad, and trust me, I was lucky to snag him."

"Dad? My dad is good-looking?"

Carrie threw back her head and laughed. Full and happy. "A hunk o' love, kid."

"Eww, TMI, Carrie."

"You started this convo, so don't blame me if it derailed."

As we rode home, I wondered what in the hell Doc had been thinking. He prepared me for the clothes and the questions and not making friends with the wrong people. But he forgot something big.

Females.

Hormones.

How could I remember anything Doc said when all my thoughts were in my pants?

And there was something else lurking on the horizon. Whoever took my clothes might want to take a swing at me tomorrow.

Could Wade handle that? Or would Kip, that guy that was part of the Loon Platoon, show his face?

Chapter 13

SOMETIMES TOMORROW IS JUST ANOTHER DAY

I swung onto the bus the next morning and took a seat without making eye contact with the other riders. We made the last pickup at a corner of a subdivision of McMansions, and a herd of kids tramped on.

"Scoot over, dude."

One of the Corn-fed No Necks that had slammed me at Scramble stood over me.

I slid and No Neck thudded next to me.

"What's in the duffel?" he asked.

"Coach's sweats and his boots."

"You not gonna wear 'em today?"

"I guess that depends on if my clothes disappear again."

No Neck made some kind of rocking motion. It appeared to stand in for a nod. I guess you can't nod if you don't have a neck.

He eyed my clothes, leaning over to check my shoes.

"You look like one of us today."

I plopped my head against the back of the seat and smiled.

"It would take fifty pounds of muscle and a complete change of gene pool for me to look even remotely like you. I'm a worm, you're an anaconda."

No Neck grinned. "You're starting to sound like Schultz — you got Schultz's dad for algebra? Guy went to school on a basketball scholarship but talks like a thesaurus. I like to listen to him."

I tilted my head over, giving No Neck a long, hard look.

"What? You're looking at me like I'm a Neanderthal — like I haven't evolved."

"You chunked that ball at me like you were throwing

rocks. You stole my clothes. That's kind of low-level thinking."

"I didn't steal your clothes, but I did watch 'em get snatched. I guess that makes me one of the bullies."

"That's . . . complicated," I said.

"Why didn't you make waves with the coach?"

I took a minute. "Why make waves if you don't know how to surf?"

"You scored big yesterday. You didn't narc. You didn't call your mommy and go home. You looked like a dork in those boots and you acted like it didn't touch you. That earns you a cool factor."

Factor. Was I getting a quotient?

"Anyway, for my part of it, the ball slamming and watching the clothes thing go down, it's my bad."

"Thanks." The bus thumped along. I had no idea what else to say. Finally I said, "My name's Wade."

"Most guys are calling you Alaska," No Neck said.

"Siberia," I answered without thinking.

"Sorry, I must have got it messed up. I'm Jay," No Neck said.

We chugged up to the school. "Siberia," Jay said as he got up, "you don't have to worry about your clothes today."

"Good to know," I said.

"No big."

No big, I thought as I headed for my locker. If you'd sat like a wet plucked chicken for what felt like weeks, the promise of not doing it again was more than just a pleasant thought.

I kind of looked forward to my Indiana history class because the class's resemblance to the Loon Platoon — the way most of them had either checked out or tried so hard to buck the norm — reminded me that I was heading in the right direction toward my goal of being normal. But I still understood them enough to relax and not treat them like "night crawlers," like Dave did.

A guy with a circle and slash self-tattooed high on his cheekbone approached me as I entered class the second day.

"I heard about your clothes. I can arrange to have the thief taken care of."

"That's not necessary," I said, mildly amused. I doubted he was as frightening as the people I grew up with.

He pointed to his tattoo. "That means *don't.* As in don't mess with me. I can have your guy taken out."

"Taken out? You'd kill a guy over a flannel shirt?"

The guy stepped back. "Kill! Shit, who are you? I meant beat him up." He returned to his seat, giving me a look of confusion. It appeared he couldn't decide if I was kidding or not.

Okay, I had just scared the snot out of someone who advertised hostility on his face. I had to watch my mouth and keep one step ahead of my cover story. There was no relaxing when you lived a secret.

The next hurdle was gym. I dragged the duffel from my locker and returned it to Coach Tulling. "Thanks for the loan. All washed."

"Aw, that messes 'em up," Coach said. "It'll take

forever to get the smell back in them. I hear you made quite a fashion statement."

I grinned. "Let's hope I don't have to make it again today." I left the office and went into the locker room to change. On the bench were my jeans and flannel shirt folded into a neat square. Next to them were my duck shoes.

Chapter 14
LOVING MAKES LITTLE SENSE

Doc had set me up for outpatient therapy with a shrink among the cornstalks. I had seen her before I started school, but this was my first session since meeting the beast.

Dr. Lyman reminded me of a grasshopper on a leaf. Quivering and ready to leap at any time. She unnerved me a little, but she was interesting in her antennae-waving way.

"I'm glad you feel the stolen-clothes incident was resolved well," she said.

"Don't you?"

"I'm not part of the equation," The Grasshopper said. I swear she rubbed her hands together. Do grasshoppers have hands?

"I've been accepted. It was the right way to go," I said, but her statement was softening the edges of my confidence.

"Was that your real purpose for suffering this indignity with such calm?"

What did that mean?

"You think I did it for another reason?"

The Grasshopper didn't answer.

"I hate it when you guys do this," I said.

"Do what, Wade?"

"That. All questions, no answers. I thought I had a handle on things, and now you're . . . you're creeping me out."

"I don't think I could creep you out if you were as certain about your decision as you say."

I wanted to keep my cool with her. I wanted to be Wade, not Kip. Kip was gone. I was a normal guy, leading a normal life. So why was my heart racing and my fist clenching and unclenching?

"So I should have pitched a fit?" My voice carried a sharp edge. "I should have ratted on a bunch of people my first day of school? Made enemies? You think that was the way to go? I think you're a little out of touch with high school."

"But do *you* know much about high school?" The Grasshopper's eyes bulged, but her voice stayed low.

Wade lost. Kip won.

"All right. I get it. I didn't think wearing the boots and the sweats would just show how I could be stand-up. I did it because I think I need *punishment.* Is that what you want to hear?"

I bolted from the chair and strode to the windows. I looked out so I didn't have to look at her ugly bug eyes. "I think I need to pay and pay and pay some more for setting a little kid on fire. For causing him and his parents and my dad all that pain. So, I deserve any shit that gets shoveled my direction."

I turned around to see that The Grasshopper was all

aquiver in her insect-y way. "That's good. You know more about yourself than I gave you credit for," she said.

I took a deep breath and let it back out. Moved slowly back to the chair, trying for some chill. I sat back down.

"People treat me wrong and I roll with it. Isn't that what I was supposed to learn all those years locked up? How to control my anger?"

"Yes, and it's working. There's nothing wrong with rolling with the punches. But there's a difference between accepting guilt and seeking punishment."

"I didn't ask those guys to take my clothes," I muttered.

"No. But accepting pain you didn't earn is addictive. We need to work on that issue or you'll end up with counterproductive behavior."

I rubbed my temples. I hadn't had a headache in a while. "I don't get it."

The Grasshopper leaned forward on her desk. "I mean, when things start going really well for you, you'll think you don't deserve it and seek to sabotage your own good fortune."

"That's crap." I blurted it out so loud it startled both of us. I swallowed and dialed it down. "I don't even think I get your point."

The Grasshopper settled back. She seemed so certain; she tossed out her words like they were already history. "You'll burn yourself if you get too happy, Wade. Just like you burned that child."

When I got home, Carrie was checking her e-mail. She looked frustrated.

"I can fix your spam filter so you won't keep getting all those offers for a quick fix for your wilting love life or a genuine Rolex for ten bucks," I said.

"It's not that. It's that I haven't heard from Grant in three months."

"Your stepdad?"

"Yes."

"I didn't think you e-mailed all that often."

Carrie rat-a-tatted a message and hit send. "But I sent him a message and told him we were in Indiana now. He didn't answer. That's not like him."

I sat down at the table. "Carrie, what's the deal with Grant? You hardly talk to your mom or your dad or your other stepfather."

Carrie turned around from the computer. "Mom married Grant when I was six and divorced him when I was nineteen. Her third husband died."

"Oh," I said. "So Grant was like a father to you?"

"Absolutely. Some of my best memories were at his beach house in Texas. I loved it there. Grant and I would look for seashells, and he taught me to sail and fish. He was there when I needed him and I wasn't all that charming to be around, you know?"

"Um, Carrie, I doubt he plucked you out of a ward for the criminally —"

"Just stop. That's not who you are. Not now. Anyway, don't be so self-absorbed. This is about *me.*" She grinned.

I don't know what happened right then. Maybe it was seeing Carrie so worried about Grant, and her remembering their good times . . . maybe it was because I saw for sure that Carrie loved me because she didn't treat me like a head case . . . or maybe it was just her lit-up grin. Maybe it was the stress of my session with the shrink. Whatever it was, something broke in me. When Carrie told me to get over myself and care about her . . . for some reason, I did. I let myself completely love her, for the first time, like a mother.

First it was surprised, silent tears, and then I put my head down on folded arms and shook with chest-heaving sobs that felt like they would crack ribs.

Carrie stepped to my chair. "Move your skinny butt over." I slid over a bit and Carrie perched on the chair and wrapped her arms around my shoulders. She rested her cheek against my bowed head. "Grant did this for me. Oh, honey, more than once. I don't know exactly what you're feeling, but I know it hurts." She tightened her hug a little. "Trust me, it might get worse, but in the end, it gets better. It finally gets good. I swear."

She was right. It did get worse. Just not right away. Just like the breakthroughs, the bad stuff always takes you by surprise.

Chapter 15
THE FIRST CRACK

I eased into school life. There were rich, popular kids that ruled the school, but I hung with the second tier. The utility bunch that make up most of a school's population. Decent kids, decent grades, decent athletes. Decent is good, especially in the Midwest.

I made a group of friends; I didn't sit alone in the cafeteria; I had a reserved spot with nonlosers; I wasn't considered a hostile force; Kip was further away and I was wearing Wade like old, comfortable shoes. But then I got careless.

It happened in English. I had finished reading *The Light in the Forest* and was working on my paper. The rest of the class was finishing their Poe unit and discussing the last short story.

"Wade, can you help me here?" Ms. Bales asked.

I looked up.

"Have you read and studied 'The Masque of the Red Death'?"

"Sure."

"None of these students seem to think the story is about anything but a party that goes bad. Can you give me some differing input?"

"Oh, sure," the superstud that played second string varsity quarterback while a freshman snarked. "The loony from the boonies that studied with his mama is going to teach us. Gimme a break."

I want to punch this troglodyte in the face. Clint Jons was the leader of the pack that stole my clothes on day one. But, like the khaki-clad teacher on the ward, I couldn't swing at him with my fist.

I glared the heavy-browed, short-necked, pecan-brained big mouth down and turned to Ms. Bales.

"The first thing you have to know is what was happening in Poe's life when he wrote the story."

"Be still my beating heart, a student that does more than read the assignment," Ms. Bales said as she put her hand to her chest. "Maybe Mr. Jons should rethink his remarks as hasty and possibly ignorant?"

The troglodyte closed his book and slumped in his seat. His nostrils flared.

"Poe's wife was dying of TB when he wrote it. So she would cough up spots of blood. His imagery of the red splotches on the skin probably comes from that. The red room is all about blood and, I think, fever, the fire that consumes the body."

"This is excellent, Wade, go on. Homeschooling seems to give you great insight into symbolism."

"Years of therapy does that." I was so busy pummeling

Jons with my smarts that it was out of my mouth before I knew how stupid smart can be. I saw Dave look at me, confused.

"Therapy is what my mom called homeschool — my therapy."

Shit, that was worse. I had told Dave that Mom died when I was nine. "Mostly my dad taught me, but my mom called it that when I was a kid and my dad kept calling it that." I raced on. "Anyway, the theme is about the inevitability of death. It gets us all. Rich, poor. Whatever. No escape."

Ms. Bales thanked me and started talking about the seven stages of life. I darted a glance at Dave. He was taking notes, but his forehead was still knotted.

When the bell rang, I hurried out of the room toward Indiana history. That made me look even guiltier, I thought. I was such a idiot.

A mammoth hand caught my shoulder and spun me.

"You think you're a real smart-ass, don't you?"

Clint leaned over me. Furious. He had never taken the stolen clothes episode well. He wanted me to grovel and I hadn't. He didn't like it that most of the school thought I had won that skirmish. Now I'd made him look stupid in class. Well, *proved* him stupid. He always looked that way.

"What are you smiling at, moosefucker?" Clint growled at me.

I was not going to fight this goon for two reasons: I promised Doc, and Clint Jons would seriously kill me.

"Clint, you overestimate me. Those moose are *tall*, dude."

Clint leaned in, quivering with rage. "Then how tall was your mama?"

All reason and sense fled. I lowered my head and rammed his gut. I think my head jammed completely into my shoulders, but Clint staggered back, more surprised than damaged. I used the opportunity to drive a kick between his legs. His eyes goggled, his face paled, and he collapsed with a thud.

Nobody moved. I stared down the watching circle and then stepped over Clint. "Stay down and from now on, watch your mouth. This was a lesson in manners."

I walked straight to the office.

While I tried to cool out, the principal tried his hand at fact gathering. I told him that Clint provoked the fight and I had finished it. Clint told him that there was no fight. The ice pack on his nuts was the result of an accident. How could a punk as little as Wade Madison bring Clint Jons down?

None of the watchers knew where they were at the time of the incident. Mass amnesia.

Ms. Bales did say that Clint had been baiting Wade earlier in class.

There were obviously no marks on my knuckles and no bruises on me to indicate fighting.

"So what do I believe, Wade?"

"Whatever you like, sir."

"Get out of my office. If I hear from that kid's parents, we may have to . . ."

"Understood, sir."

"Did you really take that behemoth down and come away without a scratch?"

"I was . . . upset, sir."

"Don't get upset again, Wade."

"I'm trying not to."

When I got to lunch, Dave was lying in wait. He pulled me to the side. "Hey, Siberia, you don't have to avoid me. It took me awhile, but I finally got the picture."

I stared.

"You kind of had a meltdown in class today when you talked about fever. I'll bet it reminded you of when your mom died. You had, like, a bad flashback?"

I dropped my gaze to my feet. I should tell him, I thought. This was the right time to tell him who I was.

"I'm betting you had therapy and don't want anyone to know." Dave held up his hand like he was stopping traffic. "You don't have to say anything. But don't think I'm going to think bad about you. Alaska must be pretty backward if you're embarrassed that you needed therapy because your mom died."

"It's not that way. It's just that I was a little kid."

Dave gave me a tight grin. “I can listen. . . .” Then he laughed. “I know you don’t believe I *can* listen, but we could tape my mouth shut or something.”

“Let’s go get lunch,” I said, wanting to change the subject.

“You’re talking lunch and ignoring the fact that you took Clint Jons to the ground! He’ll *never* get over that,” Dave said.

“That’s kind of what I’m afraid of,” I said.

We turned to drop our books on our regular table. I wondered if Dave could smell the guilt coming from my pores. I was a fraud. A thief, stealing his friendship.

Chapter 16
FINDING BLUE

I got through my freshman year with no other fights. Jons ignored me. Since he was a full head taller than I was, it was easy to overlook me. Absolutely Cutest and I had done the flirting dance, but she would flit close and then away. I think she sensed something in me that she couldn't quite trust.

Just before term ended, Coach Tulling asked me into his office.

"Wade, I've got an idea for you."

I hoped he wasn't going to ask me to be the football team's manager for next year.

"You'll notice most of this town's body type is made for football."

"Yup, that's a little obvious, sir."

"Well, they'd break you like a twig if you played football, but you're going to be long and lean, and with some work you'll have a nice pair of shoulders. Just right for swimming. I think if you work with the coach this summer, you'd have a chance at varsity. What do you think?"

"I think I don't know how to swim."

Coach scratched his head. "Don't know how to swim?"

"Alaska. Ice. Really cold water. Not much swimming."

Not quite true. Who was going to put the Loon Platoon in a pool?

"Son, that's a serious problem. Okay, I'll teach you to swim and then I'll put you with Coach Redmon if you want to work hard."

Being part of a team wasn't high on my most-wanted list. But all my friends played football, and then ran track when football season was over. I spent too much time alone with my thoughts. That was never good. Maybe swimming would exhaust me. Wade — he was born in the water, right?

"Coach, I like the idea, but let me talk to my parents."

When I learned to swim I learned the texture, smell, and taste of blue. The water of the pool was the blue of Alaska's forget-me-nots and it wrapped my skin in its cool liquid embrace when I dived in. It slicked against my skin like velvet as I dolphin kicked. The splash of my strokes drowned out any thoughts in my head, and I loved the flip turn at the pool's end, tucking under and pushing off, going deep and knowing no flame could ever touch me there.

I was a coach's dream. It was never a workout; it was an escape. There was no guilt in the pool, no shame in the blue, clean lanes of water.

I hit sophomore year with a growth spurt, and with weight training by the end of that year I was exactly what Coach Tulling had predicted: long, lean, wide-shouldered.

And aggressive as a shark. I attacked the water like it was the enemy. There was only one lane in the pool. Mine. I didn't swim to beat anyone else. I swam to beat myself, or maybe to beat myself up. That's how Dr. Lyman put it.

I racked up good grades, good times, and blue ribbons at swim meets. I also managed my first actual date and my first actual kiss, which led to more dates and then make-out sessions. Absolutely Cutest and I were an official couple.

The better life got, the edgier I got. So it was only a matter of time: I had no truth to feed the ghosts, and at some point they were going to demand it.

One November afternoon of my sophomore year, I came in the house, shuffling through the mail. Carrie had a letter from a lawyer in Houston, Texas.

Somehow I knew this had to do with Grant. Carrie had recently made contact. Grant didn't say anything about why he'd been MIA for so long. He was glad she was in Indiana. He was glad to hear she was married and happy. But nothing about himself. He'd only e-mailed once more before he vanished from Carrie's computer again.

I propped the letter on the table, put some towels in the wash, and pulled the stuff out to make spaghetti sauce. Carrie had taught me to make it last year, along with a few other classics. Carrie was at every swim meet; I could help her out every now and then by making a few dinners.

Carrie read the letter with a weird look on her face. She didn't say anything until Dad got home and we all sat down to eat.

"I got a letter from Grant's lawyer," Carrie said.

Dad looked up from his spaghetti. "His lawyer?"

"Yes. Grant . . . Grant died." Carrie stopped, pressed her lips together until they turned white. Then she spoke again. "I never gave him our snail mail address and I guess I didn't tell him our last name. It seems I told him your first names and lots of stuff about you, but never actually put in the last name. I just . . . it didn't seem . . ."

Dad lifted her hand and kissed it.

Carrie cleared her throat and took a deep breath. Then another one. "He didn't tell me he was sick. He didn't want me to worry. He died three months ago. It took the lawyer awhile to find me."

She handed the letter to Dad. "Grant left me the beach house in his will. He said no one else would love it as much as I would."

That's when she broke down in tears. I knew exactly what to do.

I got up. "Move your skinny butt," I said, getting up and perching on Carrie's chair and putting my arm around her. She wiped her eyes and her runny nose with the back of her hand and then rubbed it on my jeans.

"You are so gross," I said.

"You love me anyway," she said.

"Yup."

I thought about this Grant, a guy I didn't even know. He gave Carrie a house and a father when she needed one, and maybe Grant's kindness had ultimately given me Carrie.

“We need to break up,” Absolutely Cutest said as she looked at my Christmas present.

“You don’t like the CDs?”

“Don’t you think you should give your girlfriend something more . . . I don’t know, *personal* than CDs, Wade?”

“Personal? I don’t get it.” She had given me a leather thong necklace, which was cool, with a gold dolphin on it, which was cool, with “Love Lindsey” engraved on the back, which was not cool.

Lindsey handed the CDs back to me. “If these were mix CDs you made for me with songs that were important to us, that’d be different. These are just from the recently released shelf.”

I scratched the side of my neck. “AC —”

“There!” She stamped her foot. She actually *stamped* her foot. “That’s what I mean. AC. You call me AC.”

“It stands for Absolutely Cutest. How can that be a bad thing?” I wasn’t sure if I was bored or annoyed.

“Do you even know my name?”

“Sure, I do. You make sure of that. You want me to

wear it around my neck. Do you have to tag me like your gym clothes?" I yanked the necklace off and flung it on the floor.

"Wade, you're not emotionally invested enough in our relationship." She said it like she was reciting from a self-help book. And then she finished it. "That's it. We're done."

AC must have been right because I didn't really miss her that much. Dave and I foraged for dates the rest of the year. Three dates in a row with the same person was the longest "relationship" either of us had. We doubled on almost every date. He had moved from best friend to brother-of-a-different-mother status.

The dating habits of the three B's dumbfounded me. They dated only within their church. But it was sort of a round-robin. One B would date girl X, then move on to girl Y, and then another B would date girl X. When the first B tired of girl Y, the third B would date girl Z. When he tired of girl Z, he might go to girl X or

Y and maybe girl R would enter the picture. What I didn't get was that nobody was jealous, none of the girls felt used, and there were no hard feelings. Everybody thought all this handing off was normal. It looked incestuous to me.

My real love story was still the water. The blue that soothed me. No matter what happened that day, the water could wash it out of my system if I swam hard enough. I practiced longer, harder, and more often than any of my teammates. Again and again I made the water prove its value by slicing through it, kicking hard, pushing off, and diving under.

It paid off early in my junior year.

"Madison, get out of that pool. Son, you're growing a set of gills."

Coach Redmon stood at the double doors. I tread water and shook my head, clearing my ears.

"My office, pronto."

I toweled off as I headed to the office.

Coach pointed to the hard plastic chair. "Madison, I'm moving you to varsity. I've clocked your workouts for the last two weeks. Compare that to the guys I have coming back and you rack up the best time for the two hundred in the crawl and the butterfly. I'll make a final decision, but I'm thinking you'll anchor the eight hundred relay."

I draped my towel over my head.

"That's what you got to say? Isn't this what you've been working your butt off for?"

I pulled the towel off. "Sure, Coach, but it scares the hell out of me."

"Just swim like the devil's chasing you in that lane, Madison, and it'll work out fine."

I think that was the moment swimming turned from my savior to my demon. After that I poured my hyperactivity into workouts and into stroking and kicking in the lanes. I shaved seconds, not tenths of seconds, off my time. But it didn't soothe me anymore.

"Wade, I've noticed you've paced the entire hour," Dr. Lyman said. "You did that last week. And you're avoiding talking about anything school related. Would you like to discuss that?"

"I'm not sleeping, lately. I feel antsy all the time. Like I can't settle. I can't even stay in my bed. I pace around my bedroom."

"What's making you so anxious?"

"Anxious? Nothing. I'm not anxious. I'm just . . . uh, a little tense. The swim team. It's a lot of pressure." I paced a few more circles around the office. The Grasshopper kept trying to get me to open up, but all she got from me were more symptoms: the feeling of a weight on my chest, hyperactivity, and dread.

"What are you dreading?"

"I need you to tell *me* that."

"Are you afraid that life is too good?"

I punched the door of her office as I passed it. My pacing gathered speed. My stride lengthened. "Don't start that again. It doesn't even make sense."

At the end of the hour, The Grasshopper held out a prescription for antianxiety meds. It was one more pill in my arsenal, but I still found myself pacing at night, unable to sleep. I tugged my hair until it hurt. I considered cutting myself, but those swimsuits don't leave much skin to hide scarring.

I also found alcohol.

An accelerant.

Chapter 17
GOING UP IN FLAMES

By the end of January, Absolutely Cutest had reassessed and decided that the other side of the fence was not her choice of green. After a year apart, we were back together. Hot and heavy. She wanted sex. I wanted sex. But I wasn't sure I wanted sex with AC.

So when it was time to go for the goal, I backed off. Carrie had recently blown me off my sexual-assumption map by informing me that guys can be sluts. And she pretty much convinced me. Sometimes AC got mad, sometimes she thought it was sweet that I "respected" her so much. Sometimes she got weepy and sobbed that I hadn't changed and still wasn't "emotionally invested." I thought that if this kept up, AC was going to grow up and become The Grasshopper. Maybe that's what made me back away.

Sexual tension mixed with my underlying edginess had my motor revving in the red. I huffed and puffed and paced and ticked and tocked.

The B's had been getting wasted since last year, puking Friday and Saturday nights and praying on Sunday morning. They had a cooperative church friend who was twenty-one. For a small "finder's fee" he was happy to keep them supplied.

I knew from Anger Management classes on the ward that alcohol and managing anything is a no-go, so I had always passed on it. But one night we were all piled into Brett's SUV after we'd taken our dates home, and I was coming off another frustrating round with AC. Brett offered me a beer for the hundredth time, and this time I took it.

Never one to do anything slow and easy, I upended it and guzzled. It was cold and soothing as it gentled its way down my throat.

Brett slapped another longneck into my hand. "Slow down, bad boy. If you pass out, we're leaving you here."

I drank the second one slower and took a third from the cooler myself. By the time I drank it, the alcohol was catching up. Since my system was chock-full of mood-altering meds, the effect was a full-on buzz and light show.

I became an advocate.

But I was also an athlete. I had learned from the highly educated how to reign myself in. I rarely drank during the week. And I didn't let it interfere with workouts. My grades were good enough that a little slippage wasn't a problem. I'd pull them up after swim season.

The flameout started with the district swim meet. The big one. It was go-for-broke time and my head hurt. The lights over the water sparked glaring reflections that drove spikes of pain through my eyes and into my brain.

Coach stalked in front of four of us.

"Okay, the individual events are history. Madison, just because you won every one of yours doesn't mean it's time to retire. You're the anchor for the eight hundred relay. Kevin, Andy, Robby, it's your job to put Madison in position, and Madison, you pull out the win. Do that and the whole meet is ours. And I want it."

Coach Redmon planted himself in front of me. "I want this district win, you got that, Wade?" He strode away without an answer.

The bleachers were full. Screaming, cheering, and whistling. It almost made me sick to my stomach. My head throbbed in time with the chants. The whistles were full-on assaults. I couldn't wait to get in the water and drown out the sights and sounds. To be alone in the blue.

I shook out my arms and shoulders and tried to ease the tension from my neck. The hours in the chlorinated water had paled and scaled my skin and it goose-pimpled in the air.

Kevin, our first swimmer, set up on the platform, the buzzer sounded, and the swimmers hit the water. Kevin hit second and dolphin kicked hard and steady, then broke just behind the lead, his stroke smooth but robotlike. His time never wavered. He hit the wall and flipped, gaining on the leader and stroking out in his deadly precision, eating up the lead. He finished his two hundred leading by half a length, and the home crowd was nuts.

Andy hit clean, but his kick lacked thrust.

"That sissy kick of his always gives up my lead," Kevin muttered.

"Like you don't say that every meet," I said. "All he has to do is keep Merrillville or Hammond from running away."

"I'll bring it back so Wade can bring it home," Robby said.

Andy powered through, but despite his strong arms, he lost the lead and dropped into third, then into fourth. Disaster. He hit the wall after his two hundred, sobbing.

Robby had a long, stretched-out dive and a huge kick. He went after the water like he owned it.

"There he goes again. Coach is already screaming at him," Kevin said.

Robby had a habit of looking for the other swimmers;

he wanted to see his opponent. Coach screamed that the head swivels slowed him down. But I knew that an enemy in his water gave Rob the urge to conquer. He had made up two places when he finished his two hundred, and I hit the lane.

I swam to punish my body. I stretched out long, I kicked hard, and I held my breath until my lungs burned. It was me, the lane, the water, and in the end, the wall.

I knew nothing until I came up and my teammates were hauling me out of the water and hugging me. I couldn't hear anything but the roar in the gym. Finally Coach made me understand. I had passed the two leaders and beaten them by two lengths and set a state high school record.

"You're a hero, Madison!"

Coach had his district meet and a state record. I had a headache that was making me see double. Soon, Dad and Carrie were hugging me, Absolutely Cutest was kissing me, and people I didn't know slapped my back or shook my hand. The roars and cheers and whistles were nothing but pain.

I gulped down a handful of aspirin before a hot shower and my headache eased enough to officially celebrate with the team and our girlfriends (if we had any). Later the guys-only celebration with my real friends was well under way in a fallow cornfield. We had cheap beach chairs and a small fire and lots of beer and vodka. We also had weed. The B's weren't smoking, but Jay was showing Dave and me the glories of our first marijuana buzz. We were righteously trashed.

Brett held up his beer. "Here's to our hero."

"Buzz B, buzz!" Dave said.

"Cut the crap. It's a swim meet. I didn't discover the cure for cancer." God, how did that slip out of my mouth? My mother's pained, wasted face at the end of her life flashed in front of me. My headache came back screaming. I rolled the cold beer bottle against my forehead.

"The Wade man is too ugly to be a hero," Dave said, and took another hit of the weed. "Hey, I heard something tonight. But it's so ridunculous . . ." Dave stopped. "That doesn't sound right."

"Toke virgins. You gotta love 'em," Jay said. "The word is 'ridiculous,' but go on with your story, blockhead."

"Anyway, it's too ridunculous to believe for a minute," Dave continued, still not in control of words any more than three syllables.

"Just spill," Brandon said. "At this rate you're going to pass out before we hear anything."

"Anna Thompson. I think all of you dated her?"

"Not me," Jay said.

"You don't count. You're not of their religious preposition." He pointed his roach at the B's.

"Me neither," said Brandon. "Haven't been there yet. I'm still dating Jen. Brett was the last one to date Anna."

"Whatever. Anna says Brett is dating out of your prayer circle. Way out."

The dope must have kicked in because I thought it humorous that one of the B's had finally stopped incestuous dating.

Brandon snorted. "Now you see why I never dated Anna. She's mean and a gossip." He took another big swig of his beer. But Brendan lowered his bottle and stared at Brett. "Anna might be a little mean, but Brett's been pretty secretive lately. And not hanging with us so much. So, what's the deal, Brett?"

Dave waved the roach back and forth, dismissing Brendan. "You didn't let me tell you the rest. It's too stupid. Anna says Brett is doing the dirty deed. With . . ." He paused, dragged hard, held the smoke, then exhaled. "Kelley Hamilton." Total silence.

Kelley Hamilton had been one of my classmates in Indiana history in ninth grade. She had tats on her arms and legs and had shaved her eyebrows and replaced them with rows of rings and studs. She had nose rings, a tongue stud, more earrings than I could count, and probably some personal piercings I didn't want to think about.

"Bible Boy and Tattoo and Piercing Queen did the No-Pants Dance?" This from Jay. "No shit?"

Dave chuckled. "Like anyone would believe . . ."

"Believe it," Brett said. He looked across the fire at Brandon, who rose to his feet, his knuckles white as he clutched his longneck beer bottle.

"Brett." Brandon said the word low and hard. A warning.

Brett looked at each of us before he spoke; his voice was firm and steady.

"She works at the coffee shop, and I got to know her. She's not what you think. She's sweet and she cares about me. And if you're my friends, I'm asking you to be a friend to her."

As he talked and I watched his face, something occurred to me. He looked like Carrie had when she talked about Dad. Brett had found his "hunk o' love." And I knew something else. I had never felt that way about Absolutely Cutest.

"Brett, if she's your girl, Kelley is good with me," I said.

"You shut up, Wade. None of this is your business," Brandon said.

I guess it wasn't my business. But maybe it was time I helped someone. I'd fought plenty of people. I'd done worse than that. Could I be a friend?

I stood up. "It *is* my business. Brett is my friend and he just asked me to support him. I said yes. What the hell is your problem?"

Brandon pushed me away with the back of his forearm, not even looking at me.

"Brett, you had sex with that . . . that . . . slut? That embarrasses Brendan and me. It shames your parents and our parents. If you know what's good for you, you won't ever, *ever* see or talk to that . . . whore."

And Brett launched like a rocket. His head slammed into Brandon's stomach and both were rolling on the ground, yelling, punching, and kicking each other. Brendan reached in and pulled Brandon upright. Brett scrambled to his feet and landed a roundhouse left into Brendan's face. Blood erupted from Brendan's nose.

Dave was still laughing. "They're still not cussing. Can you believe it?"

Jay and I moved in to break it up. Jay locked in on Brandon and I grabbed Brett. Brendan decided to tend his gushing nose.

We got them down to heavy breathing and an agreement not to rush each other, so we let them loose.

"Brandon, he's your cousin," I said. "Why can't you let him be happy?"

"Just because your life is perfect, don't think you can tell everybody else what to do."

I was drunk and stoned and my head pounded, but I couldn't have heard that right.

"*My* life is perfect?"

Brandon said nothing. I stepped closer and said again, "My life is *perfect*?"

Brandon stepped back but jabbed his index finger toward me. "You don't know what it's like to have parents that are so strict. To feel guilty about any little thing you do that your parents or everyone in your church might not approve of. There's no future for the three of us — except marry somebody that's a member of the church and then run the family nursery. You don't know what it's like for your life to be over by the time you're old enough to shovel dirt."

Brandon picked up a beer bottle and slung it against

the rocks that ringed the fire. And what he said next set my hungry ghosts loose and gave them control.

"You've got it all. You're smart, the big swimming hero with parents who let you do what you want. Nobody made you play football because your dad and your granddad did. You lived out in the boonies where you were free as a bird. What any of us would give for your life."

What he would give for my life? I didn't know what it was like for my life to be over before it really got started? The ghosts were screaming. Not for guilt, but for destruction. I gritted my teeth hard so I wouldn't, couldn't let the words out.

Brandon pushed up into my face. "So don't tell me what to do. You have no idea what we go through while you float around being the swim-team hero. You don't know what kind of fallout all of us will suffer for this Kelley thing Brett's done."

He planted his palms on my chest and pushed me again. "Just step off."

I stepped away from Brandon and stared him down for a long minute. "You want my life? I'll trade."

A switch had been thrown.

"Wow, you have to go to church? Well, I showered with a guy that used to dismember his neighbors' pets as a hobby."

Dave stopped laughing. Jay's roach had burned down to his fingers, and now he dropped it without a sound.

"I ate lunch with a ten-year-old that stabbed his father who pimped him out to other men. Stabbed one of the johns, too."

Their faces all showed a combination of confusion and horror.

I drained my beer, reached into the cooler, and grabbed and uncapped another. "But you think I don't know what your life is like? You don't have a clue about my life. How about this? You don't even know my name."

I spun unsteadily and pointed to Dave. "You're my best friend. What's my name?"

"Wade. You're drunk. You're creeping me out, dude."

"You want to be creeped out? Listen up. My name isn't Wade. I'm Kip McFarland. I went to school in a mental ward for violent juvenile offenders. I was the youngest, and guilty of the most violent crime the Anchorage unit ever had. I was there for almost five years."

"You're making this shit up," Brett said. "And it's not funny."

Jay looked like he was searching his memory. "He might not be."

"Sure he is," Dave said. "He's just drunk."

"Yes, I'm drunk all right, but have I ever talked about a friend I had in Alaska? Do I talk about what I did there? Did I fish or hunt or have a snow machine? Do you know where my grandparents live or if they're alive?"

Dave looked like I'd slapped him. The B's looked at each other. Jay still seemed deep in thought.

"I showed up like a new-laid egg and you never asked anything except did I see a frickin' polar bear?" My voice was thick with disgust. But underneath it I was holding back tears. I knew where this was going. I wanted to throw myself in the fire and put an end to it.

Jay interrupted my rant. "My dad constantly rags

about school violence and gun control, and I've heard him say that name: Kip. But it wasn't a shooting. And the thing about him being really young . . ."

All I could hear then was the wood popping in the fire.

Brandon finally broke the stunned silence. "What did you do?"

"Do? When I was nine, I doused a seven-year-old with gasoline and set him on fire."

Dave hung his head and wouldn't look at me. The B's moved closer together. Jay's eyebrows lifted as if he'd solved a puzzle. "That's it. That was the story. Dude's not lying, guys."

"Did he die?" Brett asked.

I made my voice hard. Defiant. "Yeah, but it took him three days."

I felt it then. The change, the knowledge that I no longer had friends here. I had plowed under and scraped my life bare like the desolate field in which we sat. The air grew so heavy it felt like I was underwater again. Sounds muffled, pressure on my chest. Unable to breathe.

"Shit," Jay whispered.

"That's . . . evil," Brendan said.

"Don't you mean *I'm* evil?" I said. "Maybe you should pray for me."

From the dark glares all the B's shot my direction, I didn't think prayer was going to be an option.

"Why?" Dave asked, talking to the ground. "Why would you do it?"

I pushed them over the edge. "He had a new baseball glove and I didn't."

I clutched my beer by its longneck and slung it sideways off into the field. I was done here.

It was probably four miles to my house. Not a problem when sober, but a pretty long walk when accounting for the staggering and falling down.

Dad was still up when I got home.

"Wade?" he asked.

"Nope, Kip's here and by tomorrow everybody will know it."

"What?" Dad threw his book down and strode over to me. "You're drunk. What did you do?"

"I told them. I told them the whole story," I said.

"No," he said in disbelief, but when I didn't reply, his face flushed red and anger strummed in his voice as he grabbed my shoulders and shook.

"Don't you know that what you do affects all of us?" He let go of my shoulders and paced the room. "It was bad enough when it was just me, but it's Carrie now, too. It will all start again. All of it. The papers. The hate. Wade, you could be in danger. There are people who believe you got off too easy. People that believe in an eye for an eye. They could come here and . . ."

And Dad morphed from furious to scared.

When I saw that, my defiance sailed away. Dad must have seen the bare pain in my face.

He strode to me in two quick steps and pulled me into a deep, hard hug.

"Ah, son, it's time to let it go. You don't have to hurt yourself. It doesn't help anyway."

I didn't put my arms around him. I sagged in his arms, Dad supporting most of my weight. Had it been like this when I came out of my coma? How many times would we have to repeat this?

"Why did I do it? Why did I tell them?"

"Because you think you don't deserve to be happy." Dad pushed me back, but held me by the shoulders. "You have to learn that you do. You owe me that. I have never asked you for anything. I am asking you for your own happiness."

He guided me to bed, removed my shoes and jacket, pushed me down, and flipped a blanket over me.

"You're going to feel bad on so many levels tomorrow," Dad whispered. "And you're going to deserve some of it. I've seen the stashed bottles. It stops now, Wade. It stops or you go back into a hospital."

He reached and pulled one of my feet out and put it on the floor. "That might keep the room from spinning." He moved the wastebasket next to the head of the bed. "That might come in handy, too."

He headed for the door.

"Dad."

He stopped and turned toward me.

"I'm sorry. I'm always the one that screws up, and you're the one that has to suffer."

Dad was quiet for a beat. "Wade, the fact that you think about that is what makes believing in you a possibility."

Chapter 18
GO AGAIN

Dad was right. The next day was a horror show on lots of levels. Inside my head and out. The morning was quiet outside my head. Inside my head were steel drums and screeching things. A madman playing a violin? I hung over the toilet for a good part of the morning, too. Between heaves, I heard Dad and Carrie whispering. It sounded urgent.

Carrie brought me juice and aspirin when she figured I could hold something down. "So you punched the self-destruct button?" She stood with her arms crossed over her body. Not a good sign.

"I did. Just like the shrink said I would."

I took the aspirin with one swallow of the juice. I put the glass on my nightstand. "I don't think any more juice is a good idea right now."

"I kind of think hangovers are poetic justice," Carrie said.

The grim details of my heaving came to mind in full color. "Justice, maybe. But I can't find any poetry."

"Try not to stay in bed all day." Carrie turned to leave.

"Carrie, I think there's going to be collateral damage that goes along with what I did last night. I'm sorry."

She tried for a smile. "Maybe it won't be so bad. It was a long time ago, in another place. These people know you as someone completely different. Let's hope for the best."

Hope started to collapse a few hours later. Usually my phone rang constantly on Sundays. Today it didn't ring until three. Dave.

"Hey, Dave."

"Hey."

It was the first time he hadn't called me "Siberia" when I answered the phone. He didn't call me anything.

"I sorta need to talk to you," Dave said.

"That's sorta what you're doing," I said, going for cool and missing by light-years.

"Face time. Private face time."

"Sure, come on by," I said. I knew what was coming, and I would make it as easy for him as I could. Dave had been good to me from minute one, and I had lied to him from that same minute.

I waited on the porch until he drove up.

Dave waved me over to the car. "Hey."

"You can still call me Siberia."

Uncomfortable silence.

"Can we sit in my car to talk?"

I slid into the seat of his Jeep Cherokee.

"Was it true?" Dave gripped the steering wheel, his

knuckles white. "Or were you just drunk and . . . I don't know . . . spouting shit to keep the B's from killing each other?"

He wouldn't look at me, but his voice begged me to give him an answer he could live with.

I pushed my hands under my thighs and my head back against the headrest. "You know the answer, Dave. Don't make me lie to you any more than I have."

He released the wheel and rubbed his hands against his face, then against his jeans. He didn't know it, but The Frown had taught me well. He was wiping me away.

"You . . . you've been lying to me since we met?" He banged the steering wheel with his fist, then looked out his window, still unable to look at me. "You've never even trusted me with your real name?" His voice came close to cracking. He cleared his throat to cover.

I gave him a minute, then talked like I was trying to get a stray dog to come to my outstretched fingers. "That was to protect my folks as well as me. You don't know what people did to my dad in Alaska. Our neighbors burned our house to the ground. The house Dad built.

The house where my mother died. Where I was born. Dad forced out of his job. He had to change his last name to get another one."

"Because you murdered a little kid." Dave stumbled on the word "murdered," almost whispering it, like he was showing porn to a priest.

"I was nine years old."

Dave leaned his head back and stared at the car's sunroof. I didn't say anything.

"But you did it on purpose, right?" Dave voice was defeated.

I wanted to explain it all to Dave, how it had been about the glove, that it was an accident. But if I did that, and he supported me, he'd be cut off from the world he'd known. He'd become an outcast along with me. The hate meant for me would overflow onto him, like it would to Carrie and Dad.

Dave wasn't strong enough to fight this and he didn't deserve to have to.

"Yes, I did it on purpose." No apology. No explanation.

"You were in jail before you came here."

I waited a beat.

"Sort of. It's complicated. It's a mental hospital ward. But it was a lockdown ward for violent juvenile offenders. I was committed there. I couldn't leave until the court let me."

Dave looked straight ahead. Away from me. Down the road. "I don't hate you. I don't. I've loved you like a brother. But . . . I've turned it upside down and inside out. And I know that . . ." Dave stopped. His hurt had sound and texture.

"I guess you're, like, rehabilitated or something now." He stopped again. Sighed. "But I can't be the best friend of a murderer."

Another awkward pause.

He rubbed his forehead with the heel of his hand. "I don't think you're some kind of crazed killer. But I can't chase the picture of you burning a little kid out of my head. I can't look at you without seeing that picture."

"I get that," I said.

Dave closed his eyes like he was in pain. I wondered if

arguing with him, acting like an asshole would have let him off the hook easier. All I'd left him with was sad and it stripped him raw. If I were a real friend, I'd pick a fight so he could push the sad out and let the mad fill up the hole. But I was too worn-out right now to fight.

"Just so you know," Dave said. "Jay ran his mouth. He called Lindsey. She's, like, hysterical. Brandon told everyone at church and there's trouble. I'm not going to be part of the trouble. But I can't hang with you anymore, either."

"You were cool to tell me face-to-face. Thanks for that."

Dave cranked the ignition. "I have to go."

I got out and walked to the house without looking back.

Carrie drove me to school Monday and I arrived to see an assistant principal spraying the interior of my locker with a fire extinguisher. Furious, his face was red all the way into his receding hairline. I could see my papers and notebooks were burned; the books were scorched, then ruined with foam. Atop the whole mess, there was a partially melted plastic doll. The AP slammed the locker door and BABY BURNER scrawled across it in heavy black marker made the whole thing clear to the slightly stupid among the crowd.

"My office, Wade — now!" the AP barked. "The rest of you, get out of my sight. Get to your classrooms and learn something."

The AP parked me in his office and left. When he came back, he waved me into the conference room. The principal, Ms. Martin; Coach Redmon; Dr. Eastland, the superintendent of the district; and a guy in a suit were there.

"Sit down, Wade," Dr. Eastland said. "We've called your stepmother and father and they're on the way."

Dr. Eastland, Coach, and the Suit talked in low voices for a bit and then openly about school-board elections until Carrie and Dad arrived. Everyone was introduced and seated.

Coach Redmon started. "Wade, your relay teammates came to me yesterday afternoon. They've refused to swim in the Bi-District meet if you're on the relay team." Coach looked at me as if he'd hoped he'd said enough. I wasn't going to make it as easy for him as I had for Dave. I stared at him.

Coach cleared his throat and continued. "The team realizes that you won that event for them and would probably do it again, but they also realize that you'll be getting scholarship offers from colleges later for swimming. They don't want to support you in that kind of reward."

I always thought it was just the lane and me out there, but I was wrong.

"Are you throwing me off the team?"

Coach looked at the principal and then Dr. Eastland rather than at me. "The boys have their parents' support."

Carrie moved forward in her seat. Dad put his hand on her shoulder. I guess he knew when the battle was already lost. Dad and I exchanged a glance.

I looked at the guy in the suit. "He's a lawyer, right?"

Nothing. Asked and answered.

"You can't throw me off without threat of a lawsuit my parents might win. So you want me to make it easy."

"Wade," Coach said. He closed his eyes and sighed. When he opened his eyes he stared at the tabletop. "If you swim, you'll be the only member of the team."

I thought back to when Coach Tulling had called me a whole different kind of fish. Well, I wasn't a fish anymore. I'd never swim again.

"Coach, keep your team. I won't be back to the pool."

Coach Redmon gave me a clipped half nod. The worst part was that he looked relieved, not embarrassed. Not the littlest bit sad to lose me. He shoved his chair back and left without offering to shake my hand.

"Let me cut this short," I said to the rest of the group. "Nobody wants me here. You've gotten calls from the McMansion parents and that makes you uncomfortable. You're about to put pressure on my mom and dad to take me anywhere else but here. The Suit is here to cover your ass." The only eye contact I got was from the Suit.

"Done. Consider me homeschooled. Print out the papers." I looked back at my parents. "Dad, I'd appreciate your signing them."

It got worse. The newspapers got the story. I'm sure I had a civil rights case, but since I gave out the information in the first place, maybe not. Jay, Brandon, Brendan, and even AC were interviewed. Leads ran in huge print about the CHILD MURDERER IN OUR TOWN, over stories about me coming to Whitestone straight from a mental facility. Every gruesome detail was rehashed. I was the subject of sermons. Everyone had an opinion about me. Only the bad ones made print.

Dad was an operator at a chemical plant. His coworkers filed complaints stating that they didn't trust him around flammable products. They asked that for their own safety they not work on his shifts. He couldn't be fired for cause. None of it was legal, but Dad had been through this before. When a place doesn't want you, there are ways to make you leave. You get a better recommendation if you make it easy.

Carrie taught third grade. The parents of her students went to the school board. She was put on leave. Our house was vandalized. Egged, tagged, trash dumped on the lawn and burned. There were death threats on the phone and in the mail.

"We're moving to Texas," Carrie said. "To my beach house. I found a job at a bookstore in Lake Jackson. They hired me over the phone. And there are chemical plants in Freeport. Your dad can probably get a job there. Why stay here? I love that house. I love the beach. You'll love it, too."

I doubted I'd love it. I didn't care where we went. It didn't matter. As long as it wasn't here.

I had a final session with The Grasshopper. I needed a reference for a shrink in Freeport.

"So you finally did it, didn't you? Set yourself on fire?" she said as she handed me a slip of paper.

"Pretty much."

"Why? Were things going too well?"

I got a little hostile. "Do I have to hide forever? All I did was tell my friends who I am and what I did, and they turned out not to be friends at all. They don't want anything to do with me. And the whole narrow-minded town turned against my parents, too. Is there no forgiveness anywhere?"

"There's forgiveness. But you have to ask for it. And first you have to ask yourself for it."

"I hate that crap. That's TV psychobabble. I shouldn't even have to pay for this session."

"You shouldn't have had to pay for any of them. You didn't get much from them." She tucked her elbows close to her sides like she was folding her insect wings. I walked out.

We left with no good-byes. We lost our security deposit for breaking our lease. Like the landlord would have wanted us to stay and have his house repeatedly vandalized.

We filled Dad's truck and a U-Haul, and I alternated riding with Dad and Carrie. Carrie kept talking about how glad she was to go live at the beach, and never once mentioned that working in retail would be a step down from teaching, which she loved. Dad kept talking about new starts and how he'd never liked Indiana much any-way. "From religion to sports, it's too darn organized," he'd said.

But I knew the truth. He was tired of being uprooted. Tired of worrying about me. Tired of being tired, I think. Always waiting for the other shoe to drop. And knowing that I was going to drop it.

Hell, throw it.

PART III
TEXAS

Chapter 19
DÉJÀ VU WITH A TWIST

Carrie considered any driver ahead of her an affront. She crowded his bumper, then swung out into the next lane, pedal to the metal, swerved back to "her" lane, all the while carrying on casual conversation. Dad and I were used to this and had packed the back of her Honda with household linens. The only fragile things in her car were the Homo sapiens. I buckled in because I knew Carrie expected it. I didn't much care about my own physical safety.

Carrie alternately gunned and braked the car as she chatted up beach life.

"I'll teach you to sail if the Hobie cat is still in the shed."

"What's a Hobie cat?"

"Great little catamaran with no dagger boards. You can launch it right off on the beach, sail it right back onto the sand. It's a real rush. I wonder how you'll feel flying over the water instead of through it?"

She looked at me. I pointed her back to the highway. I'd told Dad and Carrie that I'd never swim competitively again. No pools, no lanes, no teams. No water the color of forget-me-nots.

"Sounds good," I said. Nothing sounded good anymore. I was phoning in a little enthusiasm because Carrie was so pumped.

"Still sure you want to study at home?"

"Carrie, I might be able to put myself through another try at school, but if it went wrong . . . I'd be putting you and Dad through it again."

"Wade, we —"

"Dad says I owe him my happiness," I interrupted,

not wanting to hear another reassurance of Dad and Carrie's unconditional support. Unconditional support was too much of a burden. I just wanted to be left alone. "Staying away from people, high school, is the only way I could even get close to happy."

"What about therapy?"

"If you guys want me to, I'll go."

I slumped down in the seat. "But I'm out of chances."

I'd burned through any luck I might have had in Indiana. The local rags ran my story, but dropped it with a suddenness that was mystifying. Nothing about me appeared in the national papers or on television. The American Civil Liberties Union seemed to have been waiting for something like this to happen. Doc Lyman had them on alert. I was still a minor when I talked. I was a minor when I committed the crime. My records were sealed. If the national news released my name, there *was* a civil suit waiting to happen. We could go to Freeport with little chance of discovery.

"Wade, I think you still have chances. Options for a

good life. A happy life. But you do have to continue therapy so you won't self-destruct again."

Carrie let that sink in for a minute. Her voice wasn't optimistic when she continued. She had a take-no-prisoners tone. "Your dad can't do this anymore, though. Keep moving. Losing jobs. Feeling all that hatred. And I don't want to lose this house. It's something that's mine."

Something that's mine. Would I ever feel a sense of possession? Is that what was missing in me? The only thing I had was guilt, and I didn't want it.

"Like I said. I won't be in school, I won't be drinking, and I learned my lesson. You can relax, Carrie."

I turned on the radio and closed my eyes, but Carrie's speed-and-brake school of driving wasn't conducive to sleep. I sat back up. She snapped the radio off.

"There's something I was always curious about," Carrie said.

"I never like the way that sentence ends," I said.

"Why you never wanted to drive."

I frowned. "I thought you'd get that. You're pretty perceptive. Dad gets it."

"Sorry, missed the clues," Carrie said.

"I was afraid."

"Afraid? It's not that hard."

I shot her an incredulous glance. "Carrie. Think. Me, behind the wheel of a powerful machine. A machine that can kill easily. Me. Known to make bad choices. Now, think about me getting pissed off at someone while driving a car."

"Oh," Carrie said.

"I'd rather ride the bus or bum rides than add that to my list of things to worry about."

"That makes sense. I'm sorry I didn't understand," Carrie said.

I flopped my head over to look at her. "Road rage. It's almost funny now. I don't have the energy anymore to 'rage.' I hardly have the energy to put one foot in front of the other. I can't get stirred up enough to give a huge wallopin' shit about anything."

I sounded so whiney that I expected tears to form in my eyes, but I guess I didn't have the energy to produce them.

We drove for more than an hour in silence. I watched the scenery flicker by like when the bored Loon Platoon used to punch the remote, endlessly seeking something to reconnect them to the world.

Finally Carrie said, "I think you would like sailing." I guess she sensed I was drifting too far away and wanted to reel me back close to her. "It's a good way to learn about physics and math. The geometry of waves, the anatomy of shells, sea life in tide pools, clouds, weather patterns; it will all be fun with it right there in front of you." She raced up on a car bumper, while gesturing with one hand toward the windshield.

For a moment, it struck me as utterly amazing. Carrie was still trying so hard to salvage me.

"Carrie, you drive like a maniac, so I think I need to say something right out loud before you run us into that old man's glove compartment."

"What's that, sissy?"

"I'm glad that Dad found you and had the good sense to grab you and hold on tight."

Tears misted Carrie's eyes and she cleared her throat. "Don't practice your flirting skills on an old married lady. Find your own girlfriend."

"Like that's gonna happen," I muttered.

But it did. It did happen.

He's talking about me, I thought. This is where he comes to Freeport. And meets me.

I couldn't read more right then. I stacked all the notebooks on the floor next to my bed and crawled under the covers. The rain was still coming dawn, pelting the windows and drumming on the roof.

Something Wade had written drummed in my head like the rain. That he was a thief who had stolen Dave's friendship. Hadn't he done the same to me? I had trusted him. I had told him my story. My shameful secrets.

On the other hand, I hadn't offered up my past until I knew the gossip had gotten there first.

I crawled out of the covers and went to the window. I couldn't see anything but the dark.

I had told him that I was through atoning. But how does someone stop atoning for killing a child? *How could I ever look at Wade and not see him as a murderer? See him standing there while a child screamed, covered in flames? Dave couldn't. I don't think anyone could.*

I needed to sleep. I needed to gather some courage to read the rest of the notebooks, to read what Wade thought of me.

Could I ever speak to him again? Ever?

And if I did, what would I say?

What could I possibly say?

I was riding with Dad, recapping my discussion with Carrie about driving.

"Like it or not, Wade, you're going to have to handle your fears about driving. There's no bus that comes out to the beach. You need to get mobile."

"I can deal with it now. I won't have high school or swim team. Or friends. I'll be okay."

Dad tried to smile, but his face was tight.

"Dad, there's something else Carrie and I talked about."

"What's that?

"About me keeping my mouth shut."

Dad clenched the wheel. "I don't want you to think we're ashamed of you. We're not. It's never been that. You were a child, Wade. You didn't understand. Hell, it was as much my fault . . ."

"Dad, don't. Seriously, I feel worse when you try to take the blame."

"Wade . . ."

"The thing is, I understand that I can't tell anyone. When I do that to hurt myself, I hurt you guys worse."

"It's important, Wade. We understand what happened to you all those years ago. We understand what you go through now. But other people don't. They can't, or they don't want to try, or they're just scared. But once they hear about it, they just see a problem they want gone."

"And you're tired of leaving."

Dad's face looked older than it should. Lined with

pain and constant worry. "I am, Wade. I'm tired. It's like there's been all this loud noise on the radio and I want to turn it off for a while."

I nodded and looked straight ahead. Then Dad realized what he had said. "Wade, *you're* not the radio. That's not what I meant."

But I was. I was that loud radio, constantly blaring.

Carrie had taken the lead, and we were following, and when we hit the top of a tall arched bridge we saw the Gulf of Mexico.

"It's not blue," I said. "The water, it's not blue."

"Yeah," Dad said, "more green. Not real clear either."

He sounded disappointed.

Not me.

We turned left after the bridge and followed Carrie a good way down a road that paralleled the beach, then she turned right and into a driveway made of crushed shells.

The house stood on stilts, with the bottom part closed in by screens, one section completely boarded. I guessed that was the shed Carrie had mentioned. A long flight of stairs ran up to the white house with green shutters. The paint was in pretty bad shape, but there were baskets of bright flowers hanging from the eaves and planted in boxes on the rail of the wraparound porch that faced the Gulf.

"I wonder who did this?" Carrie said, pointing to the flowers.

"I can scrape and paint the house for you," I said. Anything to keep me busy, away from other people. Something to punish my body so my mind stayed numb.

Carrie walked out toward the beach. "There's been a lot of erosion," she said. "The beach is practically up to the porch."

The day was windy, and all I saw and heard were the waves crashing against the sand. They made a savage kind of music. It filled my head and soothed something inside me. Had I been searching for that sound all my life?

I took a deep breath. The smell of salt and a whiff of fish, but still clean and full of life. Not the sterile smell of chlorine, but something that could nurture . . . growth? I thought I had loved the pool, but the pool had only been a prelude, a taste, training wheels. The Gulf — the unconfined, wild, fighting back power of it . . . This was the real thing.

"Well, look at that," Carrie said. She pointed to the set of white sails heading for us. Carrie shaded her eyes and the boat caught a wave, spun on the crest, flapped the sails to the opposite side, and a figure appeared. The boat sped along the wave until it hit the sand in front of us a hundred yards away, screeching to a halt. The sails let out and spilled the harnessed air.

"Now that's good," Carrie murmured.

The girl who jumped off the boat wore a wet suit, and her long brown hair flew in the wind. She waved to us, then set about securing the boat. Carrie walked toward her and gestured for Dad and me to follow.

"Hey," the girl said, pulling off a fingerless leather glove and offering her hand. "Are you Carrie? Grant's stepdaughter?"

Carrie shook the hand. "I am."

"I'm Sam. I live next door. We were friends with

Grant. He told me all about you." She pointed her thumb over her shoulder. "He always let me use the boat. In fact, he taught me to sail it. It has new sails since you've seen it. I wanted one last ride before I turned it back over to you. It comes with the house."

Carrie smiled. "No last ride. If Grant trusted you with his boat, I do, too. But . . ." I could hear Carrie's head gears spinning. "It does come with a price. You'll have to teach my stepson to sail it. I would, but I just won't have the time."

Sam hesitated, then looked back at the boat. "That's a deal I'll take." She extended her hand. All business.

"I'm Wade," I muttered while shaking the firm, rough hand. No nights of carefully applied hand lotion for this girl.

"You'll need a wet suit if you want to start now. Or we can talk wave and wind theory until it warms up if you like," Sam said.

"Why don't you come for dinner in a day or two and we can discuss that," Carrie said.

Why was Carrie doing this? She knew I wasn't ready.

"Excuse me," I said to Sam with an edge of irritation. "Carrie seems to have turned into a pimp. I need to fill her mouth with sand now."

Sam stiffened. "Well, I have a boyfriend, so Carrie's out of luck. But you're stuck with the deal because I really want to keep sailing *Elton.*" While she had been so easy with Carrie, she seemed set off-kilter in my presence.

"Elton?"

"Grant loved this old Elton John song, 'Rocket Man,' and used to sing it a lot when we sailed. So we named the boat *Elton.*"

"Wouldn't it make more sense to call the boat 'Rocket Man?' It came out more sarcastic than I'd intended. I sounded like one of the Loon Platoon.

"To you, maybe." Sam turned to Carrie. "Go see the house. I have the extra key and I cleaned it up. I'll wash the boat down, trailer it, put it in the shed, and bring you the keys later. I have a class soon or I'd help you with your stuff."

"Class?" Dad asked.

"Local junior college."

Not only did she have a boyfriend, but if she was taking classes at the junior college, she was too old for me. She didn't look that old. She looked like . . . well, as Carrie would put it . . . a hunk o' love.

The wind and waves and the green water were perfect. That boat surfing the crests — perfect. She was . . . beautiful, full of attitude, and . . . perfect.

And she didn't seem to like me one bit.

Perfect.

Chapter 20
MAYBE, THE HAPPY

We clomped up the stairs. There was a screen door in front of the wooden door that Carrie opened with the key. The main floor was one big open room. Kitchen, dining room, living room, totally open with windows everywhere, making the Gulf seem part of the furniture. I'd never lived anyplace this nice.

I was getting more miserable by the second.

"There's a half bath, behind the kitchen," Carrie said. "There're three bedrooms and two full baths upstairs." An open staircase with treads that seemed to float ran along a side wall. I trudged up the stairs and checked the bedrooms. I left the master with its adjoining bath for Carrie and Dad, skipped the smaller room next to theirs — they wouldn't want to hear my music and I didn't want to hear them.

The only other bedroom faced the Gulf. I could watch and hear the waves fighting the coastline as I went to sleep and when I awakened. Maybe if the fight was out there . . . maybe I could hand it over.

I swung my duffel onto the bed. Sailboat prints on the wall. Seashell collections on shelves. And a cloth doll. Red hair. Red-and-white-striped legs.

"Pippi Longstocking," Carrie said from behind me. "This was my room. I can't believe Grant kept it like this."

"It looks more like a boy's room, except for the doll."

"I wasn't a girly kind of kid. Hated pink. Still do." She took the doll from me. "But I loved her. She had attitude."

"You must have caught some of it," I said.

"Speaking of attitude," Carrie said, "you called me a

pimp. Couldn't you have said matchmaker?" She gave my head a light thump. "What a mouth you've got on you."

"Carrie, lay off a little. I don't want to be set up. Leave me alone for a while."

She headed back down the stairs. "I think we need a dog. Dogs don't sass."

I followed. "Are you trading me for a dog or just adding one?"

"Ummm, I'm considering the situation."

"To be fair, I don't bark, I don't have fleas, I shit in the toilet, and I don't lick my own butt," I said.

Carrie put up her hand like a traffic cop. "Stop, you've convinced me to never, ever try to set you up with a girl again. It would be too cruel."

"I rest my case."

We hauled boxes and filled closets and bought flip-flops and filled out the forms for my homeschool courses. Dad got a job with a contractor that worked with one of the chemical companies in the area. The place in Indiana gave him a great recommendation because he left willingly and didn't cause them grief.

We got wired for the Internet and I hit the books again. The literature course was easy and fun, trig was impossible, economics was interesting. I had to take Texas history, which was really interesting. Geez, I learned that I now lived in a republic. I took psychology as my elective — why not? I needed a science credit, and I found Sailing: The Dynamics of Wind and Wave Motion. I signed up.

And I learned something else. Dad took me to the lonely back roads of Surfside and taught me to drive. He said I was worse than Carrie. But he laughed when he said it. And I knew that this piece of geography had worked a little voodoo.

Dad was happy. He complained that the houses here were too close together, but he moaned about that in Indiana, too. To Dad, if you could see another house with binoculars, it was too close. But that untamable Gulf, an expanse of nothingness out to the horizon, I think that appealed to Dad. He showed no interest in the boat, but he and Carrie walked the beach and he sat on the porch and watched the waves and the sunsets.

One evening I sat with him.

"You look better, Wade. Not so . . . I don't know . . . blank," Dad said.

"It's February and there's no snow. What's not to like?"

Dad cradled the back of his head in his laced fingers.

"I like the courses I'm taking. Well, not trig. But independent study — it's good," I said.

"Making yourself a cocoon?"

I didn't answer. Dad's tone implied cocooning wasn't a good plan.

"I realize you want to keep yourself and us safe, Wade, but be careful that your comfort zone doesn't get too small."

I liked my zone small and I didn't want visitors.

The next day, I dug around in the shed and found a paint scraper and a ladder and got to work. I knew how this worked. If Dad started with a warning, Carrie followed with action. I had to head that off. I'd scrape paint during the day and study at night. How could Carrie and Dad insist I find a place in the bigger world if I was productive in my small one?

I underestimated the force that was my stepmother.

Carrie liked her bookstore job and predicted she would be managing the place within six months. It was a failing business in a great location, and she convinced the owner to shift things around, open a coffee corner, and put some tables outside on the sidewalk.

"We've got new stock and I need a strong back to help me unload. Think you could stop scraping paint today?" Carrie asked over breakfast.

I took a deep breath.

"Wade, you have to leave this beach occasionally. You don't have to talk to customers. Just manhandle some boxes."

I met her gaze across the table. I assessed her smile as a no-win situation for me.

"Sure."

But Carrie was still pimping. The owner's sixteen-year-old daughter was the barista after school and on weekends.

"Oh, Jessica, meet my stepson, Wade. He's going to help with those boxes that have to be taken to the second floor. She turned to me. "Wade, this is Jessica."

"Hey, Wade," she said. "I'm learning to make all these coffees. In between boxes, do you think you can be my guinea pig?"

I nodded at Jessica, who was pretty cute, then glared at Carrie. "Where are the boxes? And there was no mention of a second floor when I agreed to this."

Carrie led me to the back. "There was no mention of a girl either. Or you'd still be scraping paint."

I hefted a box and headed for the main room, then up the stairs.

"I'll have a mocha cappuccino ready when you come down," Jessica said.

"That's great, Jessica," Carrie said. "Wade loves chocolate."

I dropped the box next to the shelves Carrie pointed out.

"This will take all day if I drink coffee after each box."

"I work until five and you don't have a way home."

"Grand-theft auto."

"Drink mocha. Make nice."

For the first time since I moved to Texas, my head hurt.

I clomped down the stairs and sat on the stool in front of the mug.

"You don't know anybody here, right?" Jessica said.

She did the girl thing of looking up through her eyelashes. Her long eyelashes. That rimmed brown eyes that snapped with life. No disconnect here. This girl was plugged in.

"No, no yet."

"And my mom says you're not going to enroll at the high school. You're going to do homeschooling? Is that right?"

"Right again. You a spy or something?" I tried for a light tone, but I didn't like all this background check.

"So, you're not going to meet anyone and you'll turn

into some kind of beach hermit without some help. Why don't we go to a movie Saturday?"

"Together?"

"Oh, God, no," she joked. "You go, I'll go, you sit in the front, I'll sit in the back, and in a few months we'll compare notes." Jessica put one hand on her hip. "Darlin', this Indiana must really be socially deficient. You need serious remediation."

Carrie appeared over my shoulder. "He's shy. And needs a little training. I thought about trading him for a dog. But we're going to wait until he finishes painting the house."

I pushed my empty coffee cup forward. "This was good."

"Vanilla latte waiting for you after the next box."

Carrie practically snatched me off the stool.

When we got to the storage room, Carrie asked. "What was going on there?"

"Since I'm sure you set it up, I think you know. Jessica asked me out."

"And?" Carrie said.

"She scared me worse than TwoFer did."

"Oh, yes, you're going back to the shrink." Carrie shook her head.

I carried the box up the stairs, Carrie dogging my heels. Once upstairs, Carrie got in my face. "Wade, you are taking that girl to the movies. You will not be a hermit. You won't lose all the progress you've made."

"Getting us run out of town was progress?"

"You made friends. You trusted people. Making friends and learning to trust wasn't the problem."

For the first time, I thought Carrie was being an idiot. "You're wrong."

"I don't care. Tell Jessica you're taking her to the movies or . . ."

I put my hands up. "All right. Just keep out of my face."

I hated the hurt that spread over Carrie's face, but . . . I was so tired of trying. Did it matter whether I was a bad hamster or a good hamster? I was still running on a wheel to nowhere. Why did Carrie want me to invite someone onto the wheel with me?

Sam came to dinner as promised. I couldn't do much more than stare at her. By my freshman year I had gotten some control over the one-eyed monster pitching a tent whenever he felt like camping, but Sam . . . I felt like I couldn't talk and make the monster behave at the same time.

She was like the Gulf. Fresh and filling up the room with the wind and the waves. Bold and full of fight if she needed it. But able to be calm and easy, lapping at the shore. Hell, maybe I was making this up. But I didn't think so.

I helped her set the table as she chatted with Carrie over her shoulder.

"Yeah, I should be in high school. A senior. But I took some time out for a while and did some home-extension work and got ahead. I graduated in December, a semester early, and started taking classes at the JC. The basics that transfer anywhere. But I'm leaning toward marine biology. The sea has me hooked. You can thank Grant for that."

Carrie put the casserole on the table. "You and Grant got close?"

"He helped me a lot when I needed help."

Sam turned and pointed, seemingly eager to change the subject. "Did you see that lamp?"

Carrie smiled. The base was made out of a glass ginger jar filled with seashells.

"I made that for him. He had a ton of shells that he said you two had collected together. He didn't have a good place for them and was afraid they would get broken. I bought that lamp and filled it with the best of the shells. It was one of his favorite things, because it reminded him of you."

Carrie had picked up the pasta bowl then set it back down. She leaned against the counter and put her hands to her face.

"Carrie, I didn't mean to make you feel sad." Now Sam looked as pained as Carrie did.

"I know. Why did I lose touch with Grant? Stop visiting?"

Sam looked to me then back to Carrie. "Umm, Grant

told me that when you tried to visit he made himself 'unavailable.' But not because he wanted to."

Dad got up from the couch and pulled Carrie's hands from her face. He wrapped them around his waist.

"I've just put myself in the middle of it, haven't I?" Sam looked at Carrie. "When your mom was about to marry again she came down here. Grant and I were getting the boat ready for a sail. They went upstairs and talked."

Sam put her hands on her hips and paced in a tight circle. "Wow, I always thought you knew all this." She stopped circling. "When she left, Grant told me that your mom said he couldn't ever see or talk to you again. She thought he would make you sort of choose between your mom and her new husband and him."

Carrie stiffened her back and her jaw locked.

"Guess I'm understanding why I've never met Mommy Dearest," Dad muttered.

Carrie clenched her fist. "Grant was the only person who gave me time and kindness, and my mother drove him away." She didn't look like the Carrie I knew. More like the Carrie that had to run up on the bumper of any car in her path.

Then she kind of slumped. Rolled her neck. Then touched Sam's cheek. "E-mail. That's why it was always e-mail. He'd never break a promise, so he got around it." She smiled, her eyes watery with tears. "Thank you, Sam. You don't know what you've done for me. You're a terrific person."

And suddenly, Sam looked like Carrie had slapped her. She jerked back, her eyes filled with tears, but they looked angry and hot.

"I'm sorry about this, but I can't stay for dinner. Really, I'm sorry."

Sam may as well have hit us with a stun gun. We watched her flee, and the door was closed behind her before our mouths were.

Dad was the first to recover. "What the hell just happened?"

Chapter 21
HANGING BY MY CROTCH

Jessica and I settled into our seats with a tub of popcorn and our "Cokes."

"Pop is a sound, it's not a drink," Jessica said. "You order Coke."

"What if you want Dr Pepper?"

"The counter person will say 'What kind?' when you ask for Coke. Then you ask for DP or whatever."

I shook my head. "I thought Alaska was weird."

"It is. You're a Texan now, bubba."

Jessica took a few kernels of popcorn and munched. Then she turned to me, a question on her face.

"What?"

"This is a chick flick. You're either trying too hard or gay."

I pushed back against my seat. "I heard that Texans were plainspoken and direct, but this is incredible." I put my Coke in the holder and handed the popcorn to Jessica. I was here under duress, and now she was pissing me off. Time to reassess and redirect, I thought, Doc Schofield's words echoing back to me. Let the person know why she's making you angry. Be angry with the situation, not the person.

I tapped my index finger to my other fingers to count off.

"One: I was brought up to be polite. That means to think of the other person first. I thought you would enjoy this movie.

"Two: Most of the other movies are about killings, bombings, explosions, resulting fires, and have big body counts before the opening credits are shown. I don't like those movies. If that makes me a girl, okay.

"Three: I do like movies about sports. Of any kind. I think that makes me less of a girl. But none are playing tonight.

"Four: The woman in this movie is hot. Let's cross gay off your list.

"Five: I gave up trying too hard awhile back. Didn't work for me."

Jessica put her hand up and counted on her fingers. "Let's see. Not gay, not a girl, and gave up trying too hard." She grinned. "Open." She pointed to my mouth. I opened. She tucked some popcorn in. "Now, let's see if he likes popcorn."

She tipped her head to one side. "I was being a twit. Sorry. Too used to rednecks, I guess. Let's have a good time. The guy in this movie is hot, too."

She passed me the popcorn tub. "He kinda looks like you."

So, fine, I didn't have to be a complete hermit. She still wasn't going to rent space on my wheel either.

Sunday morning I awoke to find a wet suit hanging over my desk chair. I smelled the bacon and the coffee, so I hauled down the stairs.

"What are you two doing? These puppies are expensive."

Dad smiled. "I got a job right away. The house is free. Carrie says winter sailing is not to be missed."

Carrie nodded. "Take it as my thanks to Grant. I'm hoping someone else will love the Gulf like he did."

"Okay, you guys indulge me. But thanks, Grant."

"Sam is on her way over," Carrie said.

I paused. Sam. I could spend time with Jessica and never engage. Sam was different. She intrigued me.

The girl clearly had problems of her own, I reminded myself. I didn't need that. But the wet suit was bought. Maybe I could learn to sail in one lesson.

Dad appeared in my room as I slid into the wet suit. "Have fun today."

"Sure."

"Wade, we want you to make friends and Sam seems

like a great kid . . ." Dad was clearly uncomfortable. "But she's right next door and you'll be together a lot . . . and you might tend to . . . talk. Maybe you should . . . play it cool a little. You know what I mean?"

"I'm ahead of you, Dad. Don't worry. I won't be telling any secrets. Especially since she seems like she's got baggage of her own."

"Come on, landlubber, get your rear in gear. We've got a great onshore breeze."

I came out in my wet suit. "I look like a penguin."

"Nope, too tall. You look like a guy in a wet suit. All that height and the big shoulders are really going to do you some good when we ride the wire."

"Ride the wire?"

"You'll see. It's the best part of Hobie Catting."

She was the Sam of "before the meltdown" as she opened the shed and directed me to help pull the trailer to the beach. No explanations, no comments. Which was more than fine with me.

We "stepped" the mast, seafaring lingo for putting

the mast up. When the boat was on the sand we got mainsail, boom, jib, and "lines" (not ropes, ropes are for cows, lines are for boats, keep it straight) in their proper places.

Sam licked her finger and told me to do the same. She held her finger up to the air. "Feel the wind? Where's it coming from?"

"Toward us. From the Gulf, toward the beach."

"You get a star. That's called an onshore breeze. We *love* an onshore breeze. It's a beginner's dream."

"I'm ready. Let's go sailing."

"Not yet. Put on your gloves."

"C'mon, Sam. Those things are ridiculous."

"After handling those wet lines, your palms will look like hamburger. You don't get on the boat without them. Put 'em on now."

"Glove Nazi," I muttered. I put on the gloves with no fingertips. Sam whipped out a marker and grabbed my right hand and printed a big S on the back of the glove, then grabbed the left and printed a P.

"Starboard is the wind coming from your right, and

port is wind coming from your left. Bow is forward or front of the boat and stern is the back."

Before I could say anything, do anything, Sam handed me a life jacket.

"Don't need that. I swim like a seal."

"Not when the boom has smacked you unconscious."

I knew not to argue. I put on the jacket.

"What is that?"

Sam was holding what looked like a diaper with a big metal hook on it.

"Harness. It's what you use to ride the wire. You step in, snug up the ties, and you hike out and hook this in the metal thingy on the wire so you can swing out over the water and balance the boat when the hull flies up."

I pulled on the harness. The metal hook rested right about crotch level.

"I'm going to hang over the water from a wire *by my crotch*?"

"Yeah, it's awesome."

"I'm going to die."

"Well, sure, someday," Sam said.

We pushed the catamaran out until it floated. "Jump on there, grab the jib line, and be ready to haul it in when I say 'go.' "

I did. She hopped on after me, hauled in the mainsheet, and shouted "GO!"

I hauled in the jib; Sam locked the rudders down and turned them at a forty-five-degree angle to the wind. "Hang on, we're going over this big wave."

Hang on? To what? I saw Sam push her feet under some loops sewn into the trampoline on the deck of the boat, but before I could do the same, the boat shot out over the crest of the wave and banged into the trough behind it.

The boat kind of fell out from under me and I crashed down on top of the aluminum side bar, my knee catching the jib cleat.

"What was that?" I shouted.

"That was the worst part. The rest is nirvana."

I didn't know if I was thrilled or scared. I do know this girl could have taken on the entire Loon Platoon barehanded.

"I'm going to tack through the wind," Sam shouted. "Watch your head; the boom will swing over. When it does, release the starboard jib cleat, move to port, grab that cleat, and haul it in."

Carrie was right. This was school.

But when it was all done, I didn't have a concussion, and the catamaran wasn't bucking the wind and water. It slicked through the glassy green water with a silver-cool ease and speed that made my heart thump. Sam called it a broad reach.

I scooted back beside Sam. My heart thumped a little harder. When she was out of reach and giving orders like a marine I was kind of okay, but in touching distance . . . I had a physical reaction to the girl.

We sailed the rest of the morning. I took the helm a couple times. I even went out on the wire, with Sam holding my hand to help. I wondered if I had ever had such a perfect day.

Perfect.

I couldn't let that happen.

Chapter 22
THE LONG SPOONS

"I'm Dr. Martin. Sit anywhere. I've read your file. I've talked to Dr. Schofield in Anchorage, and" — he flipped though my papers — "your doctor in Indiana."

"Dr. Lyman." I sat in the chair across from his. He didn't sit behind a desk. I knew how to interpret this. No barriers here, Wade, my lad. Just us guys, chatting the chat.

"Poor woman," Dr. Martin said. "What a crappy name for someone in therapy. How can anyone trust a doctor named 'Lie Man'?"

Okay, maybe I was going to like this guy. He was pudgy with thinning blond hair, but he cut it short on top rather than try for the ridiculous comb-over.

"So, you're here because you screwed yourself over in Indiana, right?"

"Wow," I said. I felt like he'd punched me.

"That's not what happened?" he asked.

"No, that's exactly what happened, but I'm not used to the approach."

"You want me to ask leading questions and kind of coddle you along?"

I thought a long minute. "No, I don't think I do. It hasn't worked all that well for me so far."

"That's what I'm seeing in the file," he said.

I sat. I didn't know what to do with this. This was therapy turned on its side.

"What's your goal, Wade?"

"To be happy," I muttered.

"Bullshit."

I stared.

"You had happy. All wrapped up in a bow. Star swimmer. Lots of friends. Cute girlfriend. The works. And you threw it away. At a campfire, I might add. You're so scared of happy it makes you crap your shorts."

"Excuse me?"

"You heard. What's your problem? What's with the self-destruct?" He thumped the file. "Look at the size of this puppy. You've had way too much therapy not to know what you did to yourself. You even know how to avoid it. So what the hell were you doing that night?"

This bozo wanted to test me? I could test, too. "I was feeding a hungry ghost."

"Oh, that Zen stuff," he said, like this was from *Shrink School for the Seriously Stupid*. "Well, if you're gonna go the mystic route on me, remember you gotta feed a ghost truth. With the long spoons — you know that part?"

Shit.

"Didn't think so." He pitched my file on a small table by his chair. "Here's how it goes. The ghost has the truth set out in front of him in a bowl, all ready for him to eat. And he's screaming for it, he's so hungry. But the only thing he has to eat it with is a long spoon. His arms are too short for him to get the truth into the spoon and then into his mouth. So he finds another ghost with the same problem and they sit across from each other and . . ."

"Feed each other," I whispered.

"Gold star. Now, since I'm thinking you might be a little dim," he thumped the thick file again, "what's this tidy metaphor mean to you?"

I shrugged.

"I hate that teenage shrugging crap. Think."

I didn't know if I wanted to hit him in the head for annoying me so much or hit myself in the head when I had the eureka moment.

"Everybody needs help."

Martin snapped his fingers. "I officially have hope for you. And an assignment. Stop looking forward, and look back for a few days. You think you don't deserve anyone's respect. Check out the people that have stood behind you. Had your back. Knew what you did and still treated you like a human being. Make a list. Can you be so awful if those people support you?"

And that was it. Not boo or scat. He pointed to the

door and waved his hands in a shooing motion. Fine by me. Crap my shorts? Was he supposed to talk to patients that way? TwoFer would have gutted him and filed his intestines in a drawer. If Cowboy were still alive he'd have target practice with him, and Slice 'N' Dice would have . . . God only knows. But I hadn't done anything. I hadn't struck a match or doused him with gasoline. My head hadn't even throbbed.

Carrie had lent me her car, so I drove back to the beach house and booted up the computer. I Googled as much as I could and found out a few things about the Loon Platoon, then called Doc Schofield.

TwoFer had been released, only to be killed by the police while he was stabbing the second person of the night in a gay bar. Slice had been transferred to adult prison after he attacked an orderly with a shank and cut off the man's ear. The tough guy that had torched his sister's cat went home on a weekend pass and set his parents' house on fire. His whole family died. Now he wouldn't have to ask anyone what it felt like to burn a person.

We talked a little more and Doc got downright tickled

when I told him about the new shrink and his attitude. "Wade, when you make the list of the people that would stand behind you, have your back, or whatever — make sure my name is there. And not because they paid me to take care of you. Think about the kids we just talked about. I wouldn't stand anywhere near them without a guard."

I walked outside and sat on a deck chair, watching the waves. Sam drove in from her classes, waved, and walked over. Plopping herself in the chair next to mine, she slouched down, propped her feet up on the railing, and stretched her arms out behind her to cradle her neck. I didn't think I'd ever seen a person so relaxed. And it was the first time I had seen Sam so relaxed.

"Deep thoughts?"

I nodded.

"Want to talk about it?"

I did, but how could I tell her part of the story without telling the heart of it?

"Complicated," I said.

"What isn't?"

"I don't know you all that well to be having personal conversations," I said.

"True, but you look like you want to talk, and sometimes a stranger is more objective. How do you think shrinks stay in business?"

She had a point. Had Sam been to a shrink?

I thought some more. How could I get to what was bothering me without telling her? I was good at cover stories, so why not? "I was online checking out the local paper from the town I used to live in," I said. "A guy I was friends with — not good friends, but friendly — got in some serious trouble. Bad shit. I never saw that in him."

Sam shifted her arms and crossed them over her chest. She seemed a little uncomfortable, but it was like everything else with me — upending the first beer, the constant swim practice — once I start . . . "Reading about it, I got to thinking. If I didn't see him heading into that kind of trouble — what's that say about me?"

I wasn't looking at Sam. I was talking to the water, but I was aware that she had pulled her feet off the rail. "I don't want to go all drama and moody on you, but do you ever wonder about yourself? If you're a bad person?"

There. I'd gotten it out. I looked over at Sam.

And the relaxed mood was gone. Sam did the personality switch she had done the night she bailed on dinner.

"I might not be the best person to talk to about that." She uncrossed her arms and rubbed her palms on the knees of her jeans. "Why do you *care* about being a bad person? Are you one?"

"No fair. I asked you the question first," I said.

"Let it go, Wade." Her voice wasn't a warning — it was a plea. But I wasn't sure for what.

"Dad told me once that if you worry about being a bad person, you probably aren't one. He thinks bad people don't give a shit," I said.

Sam sort of softened, loosened. The shade of a smile drifted across her mouth. "I like that." She eased back in the chair again, but rewrapped her arms across herself. "I want to believe it. Your dad's a smart guy. Would he hang with a bad person?" She slid her eyes to mine, questioning.

Dad. How easy would it have been for him to dump me? Just bail when I was in Anchorage? Hand me over to Aunt Jemma? But then Aunt Jemma had bailed. It would have been easy to make me a ward of the state. But he had stuck. He'd uprooted himself three times for me, changed his name, lost everything he owned. Would he have done it if I had gone rabid like TwoFer and Slice? Why hadn't I? I had killed a child and those boys hadn't. Why didn't I turn mean? Did they feel guilt? Was guilt what saved me?

But the hungry ghost theory said I had to give up my guilt. That it hurt me and those around me. It made no sense.

My silence seemed to have made Sam twitchy.

"Let's hit the water," she said.

"Maybe that will blow the shit out of my head," I said.

It did.

For a while anyway.

Chapter 23
PIECES OF FLINT

We sailed that afternoon with no further talk except for Sam's commands. All her ease was gone, as if something about our conversation had turned her hard and tense. She drilled me about the mechanics of sailing, about the importance of the "slot" between the jib and the main, about the difference between a "tack" and a "jibe."

"Now show me," Sam said. I took control of the tiller and the main, brought the boat in-line so the bow wouldn't dig under the water.

"So far so good." Sam settled in. We were pretty far out, so I settled the boat into a reach and headed in toward the jetties, then I sailed *Elton* up and down the beach for another half hour.

"You ready to go in?"

Sam's face was tilted up to the sun. I don't know if she was watching the sails or just enjoying the warmth and the sky.

"You're the skipper."

"Let's jibe."

A jibe is a quick move and needs to be executed with the crew in sync. The boat almost pivots off the wave crest then runs down its back. It was more than a head rush. Full-body rush.

We surfed the waves, then Sam took the tiller. "You're not quite ready for the landing. Watch what I do."

As we plunged down the last big wave, Sam was watching the water, not the sail or the wind. When the waves were the right size for her, she abruptly let out the main and jerked the rudder bar forward and up. The Hobie slid onto the sand, skidded up the slope of the beach a few feet, and stopped.

"And that's the way it's done," I said.

"When nothing makes you lose focus," Sam said.

She didn't say much as we washed off the boat and put it in the shed.

Before, when we got close, I thought we were like pieces of flint, touching each other and creating sparks. Not now. We were just rocks clattering off one another.

I spent the next few days scraping paint and ignoring Sam's comings and goings. She was a complication I didn't need. When I came close she backed off. She gave no clues as to what I did wrong, how I'd messed up with her. She didn't seem to want or need me. She seemed to spend a lot of time gone. At school, I guess.

"Hey."

And one day there she was. Silhouetted by the sun in back of her. I had to shade my eyes with my hand and sweat drizzled in and stung.

"Hey, yourself." Stunning comeback.

"What are you doing?"

I came down the ladder as Sam came up the stairs. We met on the deck. "You interrupted me in the middle of my own liver transplant. What's it look like I'm doing?"

"Torturing your house."

"I'm painting it."

Sam nodded. "Gooooood job."

"Wise-ass. I'm scraping it so I can paint it."

"Looked to me like you were stabbing it to death. Must have been the angle."

She smelled so . . . clean. I wanted . . . to drink in the smell of her. Live in the color of her hair. If I kept thinking like this, I'd need to drive the paint scraper through my temple. "I don't have time to go sailing if that's . . ."

"Nope, you don't. Carrie called my house from work because you weren't picking up your phone."

I looked at the ladder then back at the house.

"Yeah, she figured you were out here 'attacking our domicile' was how she put it. She said to take a shower and come pick her up. She let you drive her to work?"

"Oh, no. Carrie says I drive like a grandmother."

"I'll bet you don't drive like Carrie's grandmother."

Sometimes against all plans of being depressed, sulky, and dark all your life, a smile or a laugh sneaks out of you. Guerrilla laughter. Happened right then.

"Nope, I can picture Carrie's grandmother going ninety and running up on a teenager's bumper and blasting her horn for him to get with the program or get out of her way."

"I'll ride with you, if you like. I'm sick of school stuff. I want a popcorn book, let my mind go on vacation, you know?"

I did know.

We chatted easily in the car, Sam telling me that I could take some courses at the JC like she did, which could count for dual credit as high school and college work. I was wondering if she was bipolar because every time we got a little close she ran away. Kind of like I did with AC. Then it hit me — that maybe it seemed like Sam ran so far because I had run the opposite direction.

The real trouble started the minute we stepped into the bookstore.

Chapter 24
FINDING OUT

"We're early. Carrie's not off for twenty minutes. I'll buy you coffee. Mochaccino. It's good here."

"Sure," Sam said, then she stopped so suddenly I almost ran into her back. Her stiffened back.

I looked ahead of Sam to see what had stopped her in her tracks, and saw Jessica at the coffee bar. One hand holding a metal cup of frothed milk, Jessica was frozen in motion, statuelike, for a few seconds. She appeared shocked, then her eyes drilled me, her anger apparent.

"Jessica," I said. "This is Sam. Straight up coffee for me and a . . ."

"Nothing for me, thanks," Sam said. She perched on the stool. She seemed more to hover over it like a hummingbird, ready to flit away at any hint of motion or noise.

"Oh, I know Sam," Jessica said. "*Everybody* knows Sam."

Jessica said it pleasantly enough. But it had that undercurrent. That "girl" thing that guys hear but can't quite interpret. She poured my coffee and slid it to me.

"I'm going to check the used section for a mystery or something trashy," Sam said.

Sam slid off the stool and took a couple of steps when Jessica said under her breath, "You can find trashy in your mirror."

Sam pulled her shoulders back slightly and her chin pointed up a little higher, but she didn't miss a step as she headed to the used-books loft.

"What was *that* about?" My coffee slopped over the rim of my cup as I banged it down on the counter.

Jessica wiped up the mess in short, angry swipes.

"I know you live next door to her, but you don't have to hang out with her. And *don't* come in here and expect me to serve her. That's shoving her right in my face."

"What are you talking about?"

"Her. Sam. Don't come in here with her. People know you and I have gone out a few times. It's disrespecting me."

"I repeat: *What* are you talking about?"

"*Sam*. She's called 'Wham, Bam, Thank You, Sam.' Do you know why she doesn't go to high school anymore?"

I moved to shake my head, but Jessica rushed on before I even had a chance.

"Because she's too ashamed to, that's why. No one would speak to her if she did. She went from being a drunk to being a ho."

I had no words. I guess Jessica could see that.

"Ask anybody. Ask my mom. Sam would have sex with anybody that gave her liquor. I bet she can't count the times she passed out and woke up without her underwear. She finally went to rehab. I think she got all her high school credits there or some story like that. Who knows? Good riddance to bad rubbish is what my mom said."

"Bad rubbish?"

Jessica leaned forward and gave me what Dave used to call the "loaded potato" look.

"Wade, you can't be friends with her and date me, too. She's a *skank.*"

I couldn't match Jessica's version of Sam with the Sam I knew.

"I'm sorry to hear that, Jessica." I paid for my coffee and stood. Jessica appeared stunned. Then her expression reminded me of Dave as he explained why he could no longer be my friend. I headed for the stairs.

Sam was helping Carrie sort a box of used paperbacks.

"Hey, kiddo, we're just about done," Carrie said. "Five minutes and then we can go. Finish flirting with the barista. Sam and I can handle this."

I flopped into a threadbare upholstered chair. "There's nothing I'd rather do than watch women work."

"Don't get used to it," Carrie warned.

I watched and listened as Sam worked and chattered with Carrie. Nothing. I knew she had heard Jessica, but aside from that slight straightening of the back, you wouldn't have known a thing.

I drove us back home and Sam sat in back, but I didn't think that was much to go on. When we pulled into the driveway, we all got out; Carrie headed for the house and Sam leaned against the car.

"So now you know," she said.

"I don't know what I know," I said. I leaned against the car next to her.

"Didn't Jessica tell you that I was a drunk and I had any kind of sex with anybody offering a bottle?"

"More or less," I said.

We didn't say anything. I stared at my feet and shuffled the crushed shells of the driveway. Sam watched the waves.

"Is she telling the truth?"

"Does it matter?" Sam asked.

I thought about that. Did it?

Who was I to judge anyone?

I turned to her and shrugged. "Actually, no. It doesn't. I'm asking because it doesn't fit. Like an outfit you'd never wear."

She looked up at me, surprise evident on her face. Maybe I was a "whole new kind of fish" for her. Some of the tension seemed to leak out of her.

"It's true. Or it used to be. Most of it. The sex stuff is exaggerated." She rubbed the back of her neck. "Like it matters if it was two guys or twenty — the *reason* you give your body is what makes it right or makes it shameful, and only you can decide that."

She watched the waves again.

"She said you were in rehab?"

"Yup. Twice. Didn't take the first time. Came out thinking I had it made, walked down the beach to a party to prove it to myself and everyone else. Got drunk on my butt. My dad drove me back to rehab while I was still hungover."

"Compulsive recidivism."

Sam shot a quick look at me.

"Sounds like you were scared to leave rehab and worked your way back," I said.

"That's therapy-speak. Groupthink. You've been in, haven't you?"

Shit.

"Had problems when my mom died."

She searched my face and I looked away. "Okay, something tells me you're lying, but nobody has to talk about their therapy if they don't want to."

She waited but I didn't answer.

Sam pushed away from the car. "You're damaged goods, Wade Madison."

She didn't say it accusingly. Just a statement of fact. But there was something else in there, too. Something I'd never encountered before.

I didn't get a chance to figure it out or come up with a clever response to her observation before she went on.

"Just so you know, I lied, too, so you're off the hook."

"I'm relieved." Yeah, there was the clever part. Sam looked at me. I think she wanted me to ask. "What did you lie about?"

"I don't have a boyfriend. I tell people that to . . . I don't know, seal myself off or something. Now, I think that's enough info for you to process right now. More later." She pushed her hair back and laser-locked my eyes. "Or not."

She turned to go, but I reached out and touched her shoulder. Sam stopped and stood still. I kept my fingers on her shoulder as I circled around to face her. I pulled her against me in a long hug, my face buried in her hair. Her body leaned into mine and one hand slid up to rest against my cheek. No words, just shared warmth.

Body language.

The best kind.

As I held her I remembered that Sam had said when we sailed that I'd get a feel for the wind, the water, and the boat. That I wouldn't have to watch the sails; I'd just know when it was right to pull the sheets in tight or let them loose. I didn't know yet about the boat, but I knew it was time to end the hug.

I eased back. She caught my gaze and stepped back without breaking eye contact, her head up, her back straight, her body at ease.

We didn't speak.

She didn't smile.

She sort of assessed me with a look just south of surprise. She blinked her eyes slow, like a cat that signals its trust, and something told me I had finally done something right.

She took another long step back while still staring at me, then turned and walked away. I waited until she climbed the long stairs to her porch and closed the door behind her. She never looked back.

It rained for the next three days. Fierce, wild storms that Carrie called Texas thunder boomers. The thunder sounded like the world was cracking in half, and lightning split the sky like a flicking tongue. The rain pounding on the roof competed with the roaring waves. I was a cocoon of peace inside all the wildness. I studied. I cooked and cleaned for Carrie and Dad.

I knew not to go to Sam.

Chapter 25
ONE LONG SPOON?

Carrie got in my face over breakfast. "Wade, what's up with you and Jessica?"

"Nothing. She doesn't want to date me anymore, that's all."

"I've noticed if I mention your name at the shop, the coffee turns to Frappuccino. I'm getting the big chill from her mother, too."

"Sorry. I didn't do anything. She just doesn't like me."

"Wade."

I looked up.

"You didn't . . . tell her, even hint at —"

"No. It happened when Sam came with me to the shop. She has an old grudge against her. Some girl thing. She wanted me to choose between being Sam's friend or hers. So I did. Relax, Carrie. I'm not going to tell."

But the time was coming soon when I would need to tell.

Sam came to me in a school-bus yellow raincoat on the third day.

The wind practically shoved her into the house. She shucked the raincoat and hung it by the door. We already had towels under the rack.

She shoved her damp hair away from her face. Sighed. Did that shoulder-straightening thing. "I need you to know it all. The whole story."

"Unless you have some confessional compulsion, I don't need to know. And *you* need to know I'm in no position to judge anyone. So, it doesn't matter."

"It might. You never know how you'll react until you

hear it all. And I won't keep secrets if this . . . we . . . are going to start."

We. There might be a "we." While my heart pounded, so did my head. How could there be a "we"? If Sam opened up her life, how could I keep mine a secret? That would be even worse than stealing friendship. But I promised Carrie and Dad that I wouldn't tell anyone my story. How could I deflect this?

I pointed to the living room. "Want something to drink?"

"Do you have coffee?"

"Left from this morning. No promises about quality."

Sam nodded. She curled into the corner of the couch, her feet tucked underneath her body.

I poured the last of the coffee from the pot and brought it to her. "I'm really fine with what you've told me. There's no need to put yourself through . . ."

"It's important to me," Sam said as she took the mug. I sat in the chair opposite the coffee table. If this had to happen maybe we needed some physical distance.

And I wanted to watch her face. Maybe she needed to watch mine.

"It was spring break when I was in eighth grade," she started. She took a sip from the mug. "I wasn't quite fourteen. My best friend, Roxanne, was spending the weekend with me, and Friday night we told my parents that we were going to the movies with her sister. My first big lie to my parents. They trusted me and went to dinner with some church friends."

"Fourteen's pretty old for a first big lie," I said. I still wanted to head this off or . . . something. Sam stared at me over the rim of her cup. I leaned back into the chair. "It's just that I did worse, younger."

Sam lowered the mug. "Roxanne practically dragged me down the beach. There were three beach houses in a row filled with high school kids. Dozens of people I didn't know milled around fires burning in sandpits, beer in their hands. The music and the people were loud.

"At the first house, a guy turned around and spotted me. He said, 'Lawd, I must be drunk. I've never seen anybody this pretty at school.' I didn't know how to handle a compliment so I blushed and ducked my head.

"He called over to his buddies, 'Does anybody know this little piece of gorgeous? Is that the cutest thing you've ever seen? Who are you, darlin'?' he asked me.

"I told him my name and he couldn't believe it, at first. 'Sam Kirksey? Isn't your dad the preacher of that voodoo Baptist church that's down the road?'

"I kind of laughed and told him it was evangelical, not voodoo. Either way, he didn't care. It was a turn-on for him.

" 'Sam, Sam, Sam. A PK. This is my lucky day.'

"He went on and on about it. Then he looped one arm around my neck. The hand that held the go cup was next to my ear. I don't think I'd ever been that close to a beer before. Honest. It smelled like heaven. That kind of smell that makes you want to close your eyes and hold your breath to keep it in, like when you smell bread baking."

Sam broke off, almost as if just the mention of beer made her have to collect herself. As if to wash away the memory of the smell, she took another sip of coffee.

Instinctively I took a sip of my own. Maybe to signal that I was with her.

"Anyway, he asked me to walk along the beach with him. I hesitated, but he reassured me. He said he wouldn't hurt me."

Sam almost grinned. "He said he wasn't 'Lester the Molester.' " She shook her head and made a face. I guess it was a gee-I-was-such-a-stupid-kid face.

"He even said that Roxanne could watch the whole time if I wanted. He just wanted to talk. Roxanne waved me off and I walked away with him. I didn't even know his name.

"We wandered toward the water and then he stopped, and turned, and put his forehead against mine. The moon wasn't out, but it didn't matter. I was moonstruck. I thought it was all so romantic. He said, 'Pretty, pretty Sam. I want you to give me a graduation present.'

My stomach clutched.

"I must have flinched," Sam said, "not knowing what he meant, because then he pulled back and put one finger against my lips and said, 'Ssssshh. I know you've certainly been kissed before, but I want you to pretend you haven't. I want to believe you've never, ever been kissed.'

"Well, I never had been kissed. I was thirteen and a PK. But I wasn't going to tell him that. He asked me, so sweet, whispering in my ear, 'Would you let me let me kiss you, Pretty Sam the Preacher's Daughter? Wouldn't that be the greatest graduation present ever?' "

Now it was my turn to collect myself. Kissing Sam. I wanted it. For some reason just her *talking* about it made me flush. But she was wrapped up in her story and, thankfully, didn't notice.

"I nodded and waited. He put one finger under my chin and lifted my face and lowered his. He kissed me. Soft. He pulled back and smiled. Then slid his hand along my face and leaned back in and kissed me for a long, deep kiss. . . ." Sam broke off, realizing that these details were ones she didn't need to share with a guy. "But what surprised me the most was that the best part of his kiss was that it tasted of beer. Yeasty, not sweet or bitter. I loved the taste — of the kiss and the beer.

"When he pulled back, I took his go cup. 'Corrupt the

PK a little bit more,' I said. 'Give me my first drink.' I sipped the beer. It was so cold and foamy and . . . *fresh*. I smiled and drank. 'Let's go get you another cup,' I said. 'This one's mine now.'

"I drank a lot of beer that night, too much beer. So did Roxanne. Thank God my first-kiss boy was a decent guy. He held my hair back when I threw up and he held Roxanne's head and mine under the outside cold-water tap until we were slightly less drunk. Then he walked us both back to my house and helped us up the outside stairs.

"I didn't expect to hear from him again. I wouldn't have known how to talk to him if I had. But somehow my first kiss and my first drink are intertwined, and it was easier to find the beer than track down a senior guy.

"So there it was. I had my first all-consuming crush. With the beer. And it just grew from there. It wasn't long before it turned into a full-blown love affair with wine, then hard liquor, but right then — it was a giddy schoolgirl's crush and it was the *only thing* I thought about."

Sam stopped talking and drank her coffee.

Sam's big secret was that she was a drunk by the time she was fourteen. I knew from my reaction to her first kiss that I didn't want to hear about the sex part, exaggerated or not. But alcohol and sex — well, if she felt so . . . *bad* about that, she could never handle my secret.

"Isn't your coffee cold?" I asked.

"Getting close, but it's fine," she said. "I love coffee. Any way, anytime. When I go to bed, I think that I need to hurry up and sleep so I can wake up and have my coffee."

I laughed. "Addict."

"Yes."

No humor in Sam's face or voice.

"Sorry, that was a lame joke. I didn't mean. Look, I used to drink, too."

"Used to drink?"

"Yes, last year. And it made some problems for me so I know —"

"And you stopped. You just stopped drinking?" Sam asked.

"Well, yeah, I —"

"Then pardon me, you don't know shit about addiction. You can't just stop when you have an addictive personality. When there's something I like, I go at it full tilt. When I was little I had to be the good kid and I had to be the goodest of the good. Then I wanted liquor. Next I went after those high school credits like they were bottles of bourbon."

As Sam talked, her irritation eased a little. I decided to shut up and listen.

"I think AA works because drinkers trade their addiction to alcohol for addiction to meetings. An addiction that's not harmful substituted for a harmful one, you know?" She sighed. "My mom can't keep chocolate in the house. I can't eat just some and leave the rest. And then there's coffee. And even sailing."

I waited a second, then asked, "Should I make more coffee?"

So much for the shutting up.

"Is that supposed to be funny?"

"No," I said. "Yes." I opened my hands, palms up. "Hell, I don't know what to say to you. I open my mouth and all the wrong words seem to fall out."

Sam put her mug on the table and stood. "I thought I had a handle on this, Wade. Thought I had gotten through it. But I can't sit here and look you in the face and tell you the worst part of it. The really bad stuff."

"Don't," I said. "Please don't go. I didn't mean to make fun of you. I'm an asshole. I'm sorry. I was just trying to make it easier." I reached out and grabbed her arm.

And she became a Sam I had never seen. Tears glazed her eyes, but she whirled, snatched her arm back, and then raised it as if she would hit me. "Don't!" Her voice was a low, feral growl. "Don't *ever* grab me!"

She bolted, grabbed her yellow raincoat, and ran out the door and down the stairs.

She didn't take time to put the raincoat on. I could see the rain soaking through her clothes before she reached her front door.

How could I be so stupid? How? I grabbed her coffee

cup and hurled it at the door. It smashed into jagged shards. Waiting for me to cut myself when I picked them up.

When I got myself under control, I measured some more coffee, dumped it into the new filter, added water, and while I watched the dark liquid fill the pot, I went over the whole thing.

Sam drank. Like I hadn't? In shrink-speak it sounded like her drinking was straight-on addiction and mine was situational. I hadn't touched alcohol since the night of my self-destruction in Indiana. Hadn't even thought about it. But it sounded like Sam sniffed the air for the fumes all the time. I guess that ease of self she projected was just a mask she wore. A lot like a fake name.

This time I knew I had to go to her.

Chapter 26
ONLY ONE BOWL OF TRUTH

Sam's Dad met me at the door.

"Get inside, son, and dry off." He chucked a towel at me. I pulled off my poncho, hung it, and dried my face. "I know you came to speak to Sam, but you'll be chatting with me first."

I'd met Sam's parents soon after we moved in. Sam got her facial features from her mom, but the long, lean DNA was inherited from her dad. He wore jeans and a plaid shirt and, with the exception of his glasses, looked more like a ranch hand than a preacher. I'd bet he could pitch me like a bale of hay. His usually friendly demeanor seemed on vacation at the moment.

What did he think? That Sam had come to me for alcohol and I . . .

"Reverend . . ."

"Wade, I know exactly why Sam went to talk to you and what she told you." He took the towel from my hands, tossed it over my poncho, and pointed me toward his study.

He sat behind a plain desk and I sat in an upholstered chair that was comfortable but looked secondhand. Their home was small, their things old and used, but it was cheerful, neat.

"Sam told you that's she's been in rehab twice for alcohol addiction," the reverend said.

"Yes, sir."

"What else?"

"She got really upset and she couldn't tell me any more."

"But you have an idea?"

"Someone told me some gossip earlier. Sam said that the gossip was exaggerated but true, so, yes, I have an idea."

Sam's father templed his fingers and rested his chin on the points. "And yet, you come here." He sighed.

He seemed to be waiting for something from me. "I said something stupid."

He looked at me a little longer. He rubbed the back of his neck. Sam's gesture. "Wade, the things Sam has to tell you aren't pleasant."

"I hear you, sir."

Her father put both hands on the desktop. "No, you don't. Sam's drinking didn't start out with her being a wounded soul trying to numb some horrible pain. We've talked about it. She loved the taste. Of beer. But then she found the feeling of being drunk. And after living in a family that was structured on religion, drunk felt free and uninhibited, and she fell in love with that."

"She told me that part, sir. I don't understand how she feels about it now."

"Now she denies that she grapples with shame," Sam's father said. "She's making progress. Telling you was a big step."

Shame. Guilt. Was that why we shouldn't keep guilt? Did it make you feed those ghosts the best parts of yourself?

"I don't know why she trusts you. I have my doubts about a young man that hides himself away, doesn't go to school, seems to say so little about himself."

He stood and came around the desk. "But it's a familiar pattern. One I've seen in this house. So, I'll not ask nor judge. But I'll warn you that my daughter is struggling, and any young man that adds to that struggle rather than helps — will not find me a friend."

"I understand. May I speak to Sam?"

"I'll ask. If she wishes to, you may speak in here. I'll be in the next room."

"I'm sorry I made a joke about something serious," I said. Sam had taken her father's place across the desk. He left the study door open and sat on the sofa in the main room.

I moved forward in the upholstered chair, perching on the edge. "And I'm *really* sorry about grabbing your wrist. If you want to tell me more, I want to listen."

She gave me that long cat-blink again and a soft almost-smile.

"What made you quit? Something had to happen, right?" I thought about Dave and the B's' shocked faces, and my last bottle of beer.

Sam nodded. "Grant had moved here full-time when I was twelve or so. We had searched for shells together. He taught me to play chess. One morning my sophomore year, I was filling a water bottle with vodka to take to school, and before I had the cap screwed back on, it hit me: The sun's barely up, and I'm going to be smashed before I hit my first class. I'm fifteen. I'm not sure how many boys I've had sex with.

"I was looking out the window and saw Grant stepping the mast for an early sail. I ran out and told him that I was in trouble. I was a drunk. I was drunk *now.* My parents didn't know. Could he help me? Then I threw up on his boat shoes and started crying."

"And Grant?"

"First he washed off his shoes. Then he called my parents and they all took me to rehab."

"And?"

"And rehab, back home, back to rehab, lots of studying, lots of high school credits, enough for early graduation. Finally back here. Grant taught me to sail not long before he got sick. I started taking classes at the JC. Life is good."

I nodded. "*Is* life good?"

She tilted her head for a long minute. I could see she was giving my question long consideration. "It is." She pointed at me with her index finger. "And do *not* make any smart remarks. I hate that my life sounds like one of those cheesy 'message movies' on cable TV about a kid in trouble."

She put her hands on the desk. Flat. Her voice was flat, too. Firm.

"If I beat myself up about the bad stuff I did, I'm ignoring that I was strong enough to stop being that person.

I think what I'm doing with my life now is a lot more important than what I did when I was a stupid kid."

I was going to tell her. She would understand. I was sure of it.

"There's one thing I really regret though," Sam said.

"What's that?"

"I wish I would have had the guts to go back to school. Walk down the halls, go to class, and hold my head high. I know I'd have been ostracized; I know people would talk, call me names, but I should have gone back and taken it on the chin, you know. The only damage I did was to myself. It's not like I killed somebody."

"No," I said. "It's not like that at all."

Chapter 27
FIGURING IT OUT

"I gotta tell you, Wade, you're getting on my nerves."

"Dr. Martin, are you sure you went to shrink school?"

"I finally got you to say something. You asked for a special session and then you sit here like a lump for ten minutes. I'm a shrink, not a mind reader."

"Am I supposed to laugh?"

"No, you're supposed to talk. What's the big hairy deal?"

So I told him the big hairy deal.

"How long have you known this girl?"

"Sam, her name is Sam."

The fool smiled and jotted something on his notepad.

"What's that about?"

"What?" Martin asked.

"Don't rev my motor. That smile and the note taking, what gives?"

"Sam, you insisted I call her Sam. Think about it. Think about the ward and your friends in Indiana."

"You been raiding the drug cabinet?"

"Wade, you aren't this dense, you're resisting." He flipped through my folder. "Who was that girl you dated for a couple of years in Indiana?"

"Absolutely Cutest." I sagged into the chair. "Oh."

"Oh, indeed."

"Square Head, No Neck, Ward Nazi, TwoFer, Cowboy, The Frown. I don't like to use anybody's real name."

"Why would you do that?" Martin asked.

I thought about The Frown. I started calling him Dr. Schofield when I got ready to leave the Ward.

"I do it to keep people from getting close."

"And he gets another gold star. Certainly it was useful in your time on the ward, but using it when you went to school shows you weren't ready to accept friendship yet. You didn't feel you were worthy of a real friendship. Subconsciously you knew you were going to blow that situation to shit before you ever started."

"But now?"

"I don't know. What do you think?"

"I hate shrinks."

"Watch it, you're gonna hurt my feelings," Martin said, wagging a finger at me. "Let's go back. How long have you known Sam?"

"Three months, almost four."

"So, this isn't true love? There hasn't been time for a real relationship to cultivate."

"No, I haven't even kissed her. But I think there could be something. A real something. A good something."

"If you don't know there's a relationship yet, why do you want to tell her everything?"

I drummed my fingers against the arms of the chair.

"Because she trusted me. It would be wrong not to trust her."

"Then trust her."

"I did until she said that thing about how she didn't kill anyone." I ran my hands through my hair. "Her dad's an evangelical preacher. I don't know if she'll think I'm evil. That eye-for-an-eye thing. I remember that letter to the editor that woman wrote, all about God and the Bible and stuff."

"Let's see . . . you told your friends in Indiana because you sort of wanted them to turn against you, but now you're worried that if you tell Sam she might do the same thing and you don't want that."

I nodded.

"Guess what that's called?"

"A mess?"

"Progress, Wade. Real, truer-than-shit progress."

The rain passed and the heat caught up. There was no wind to find in midday, making dawn and dusk the best times to sail. Sailing time was short but spectacular with the rising or setting sun. Sam in a tank suit was pretty spectacular, too. And for the first time in my life, I had a tan.

We hoisted the sail in the late afternoon when the wind was just about to pick up. We pushed the boat until it floated, and jumped on. I was manning the tiller and the mainsheet. The breeze was light and the waves were laplets that we sliced through. Slow, gentle sailing, like Sam's smile.

I tacked the boat and lazed parallel to the beach, picking up speed as the sun went down.

"Deep thoughts again?" Sam asked.

"Sort of," I said. We were stretched out, our heads propped on life jackets, and my foot guiding the tiller. Easy sailing, roiling thoughts.

"Did you really mean that you don't have any regrets? Other than not going back to school? Don't you want to just wish it all didn't happen?"

Sam trimmed the jib, seemingly unconcerned with my

question. "Are you asking if I feel shame? Sure. But if I regret the whole thing, ummm . . . well, didn't it kind of make me who I am now? If that hadn't happened, maybe I'd be one of those girls that don't think any deeper than — should my nail polish have sparkles today or be French tip?"

She crossed her ankles and flexed her toes. Released. Sighed. "I hate that my parents were embarrassed and disappointed, but I'm done . . ." Sam seemed to grope for a word. "Atoning. I can't regret who I am. And I don't. I guess I wish I hadn't had to hurt myself so much to get here, but . . ." She turned her smile on me again. "I learn the hard way."

"What if you *had* hurt someone else? Seriously hurt them?"

The smile vaporized. "I don't know. That's hard. I'm glad I didn't." Sam sat up and shaded her eyes. "Hey, we have company."

I sat and followed her pointing finger. Black fins, at least twenty of them, swam behind the boat.

"Sharks? They come in to feed at sunset, right?"

"Porpoises," Sam said. Her smile had returned, wide and infectious. "Slow down, just a little."

I eased the sails.

The porpoises caught up to the boat. They surfaced and peered at us with liquid obsidian eyes. The water foamed and tumbled as they blew, rolled, and frisked around the boat. Two small ones raced alongside the Hobie, circling back when they got too far ahead, then raced the boat again.

When the porpoises were close enough, Sam reached back, caught my hand, and tapped the flat of my palm on the back of one nudging the Hobie midships. A shiver not unlike a wet hand touching an ungrounded wire swept through me.

The sun began its trek back toward the sea.

She didn't let go of my hand.

She leaned forward and kissed my cheek and then my lips, gently, just a brush, more a promise of a kiss.

I wanted this. I wanted her. But I had to earn her first.

"We need to head back," I said. The wind had picked up and the boat seemed to spin on its rudders and the main swung over and filled with a snap. The porpoises turned with us, following, leading, nudging the sides.

One of the small ones kept popping up his head and squeaking.

"What's he saying?

"He thinks my boyfriend is funny-looking," Sam said.

Boyfriend.

I couldn't look at her.

"There's the house. We need to turn in." I pulled the rudder toward me and the boat skimmed the new-formed waves.

Again the porpoises turned as a group and followed the boat, surfing the waves. As the boat got within a half mile of shore, the rest of the pod stopped, milling in a small knot.

The two small guys still surfed alongside the Hobie, heading into shallow water. The big porpoise nosed down, his flared tail rose out of the water then slammed the surface with a crack, causing the youngsters to halt and look back. The renegades reluctantly turned and swam home.

When we hit the beach, Sam turned to me. "Clean and put up the boat yourself. It's yours and I won't be using it anymore."

"What's wrong?"

"Don't pretend you don't know. You pulled away when I kissed you. You ran this boat home like your butt was on fire when I called you my boyfriend. I don't need to be hit on the head with the mast to get the picture."

"Sam, I don't understand, repeat, do *not* . . ." But then I did understand. She thought I was rejecting her. That I might accept her as a friend, but as a girlfriend, as a romantic interest, I might see her as . . . What else could she think? She didn't know my secret. She didn't even know I *had* one.

"I thought you actually understood," Sam said.

"I do. Sam, you don't understand. I—"

"You told me you didn't judge me." She stepped away and turned her back.

"Sam, please. Don't run away again."

She didn't run. She walked.

But it was still away.

"I want to tell Sam."

Dad looked up from his dinner, stunned. "No," he said.

A flat refusal? No discussion, no . . . kindness and understanding?

"I have to."

"No, you don't." Dad slammed his fork against the table. The dishes and glasses rattled, startling us. Dad included. He took a deep breath. "Why do you want to sabotage yourself again? So soon?" He put his head in his hands for a minute, then looked back up. "You know what happens, Wade."

I glanced at Carrie. Her face was pale.

I pushed my plate aside and tried to think how to make Dad understand. "I waited too long in Indiana. That was the mistake. And how I did it was a mistake. I have to tell Sam something about me before our friendship goes on much further."

"How much do you have to tell her?" Dad asked.

"All of it," Carrie said. "How can he tell part of it?"

"Are you sure?" Dad asked.

"Wrong question," Carrie said. "Right question would be why do you want to tell her?"

I turned to her. "Same reason Dad told you."

"Wade . . ."

"Dad, I'm going to talk to Dr. Martin first. Then I'm going to write it all down. The whole story. Sam can read it. If she can't accept me, what I've done, who I am, okay. I'll leave her alone. I'll ask her to keep it to herself. I think she'll see from the story how it affects you guys if she doesn't."

I turned to Carrie. "I trust her to do that, don't you?"

Carrie sat back in her chair. "Maybe. It's a tough call." Tears welled in her eyes. "I know what you want. But we've been so happy here. I don't want to leave, Wade. You have to understand that."

I felt like I was standing on one leg.

"I won't make Carrie leave," Dad said. Now his face was pale, stricken. "You'll have to carry this one alone. A boarding school or something. I can't . . ." His voice broke. "I'm sorry, Wade. I can't do it again."

And now Dad had taken the other leg. For the first time I was walking on my own.

"You don't have to," I said. "If it goes wrong, I'll leave. It's fair. It's more than fair. But it's something I have to do."

"You have to do this?" Dr. Martin asked.

I nodded.

"Not to beat yourself up, kick the shit out of yourself, etc. and yada yada?"

"No. And you know what I figured out?"

"I hate this part." Dr. Martin leaned back in his chair. "It means I'm about to lose income or I'm about to learn what a crappy shrink I am."

"You *are* a crappy shrink. Shrinks are *not* supposed to talk. They only ask, 'And how does that make you feel?' "

"And how does that make you feel when a shrink does that?"

I rolled my eyes. "Can we get back to what I figured out?"

He opened his palms. "Out with it."

"I have to live with it."

"That's it?"

"It's pretty profound," I said.

Doc Martin didn't say anything. He gave me a go-ahead wave. "Waiting for the good stuff."

"I've been waiting to *forget* that I murdered Bobby Clarke. Or forgive myself. That's not ever going to happen. And I haven't lived my life. I've been . . . I don't know, marking time, marching in place."

I leaned in. "I figured out that I can't forget. I can't really forgive. But I can live. *Live* with it. Like you live with a scar or a limp or whatever. You always know it's there. It reminds you never to let yourself do anything so stupid and horrible and wrong again. I step out of my rut, step again, and keep stepping.

"I *live* with it."

Chapter 28

YOU GOTTA LIVE TO HAVE A SHOT AT HAPPY

I'm a rotten typist and this seemed too personal for print. I bought ten of those lined books that have the black-and-white marbled-looking covers. I holed up.

I asked Carrie and Dad questions as I wrote. I called the hospital in Anchorage, got all my chronology straight. There were a lot of nights that I cried. Especially the night Dad and I talked about Mom.

"I found her journal when I was eight. I didn't really understand all of it. But she had hidden it, so I didn't show it to you."

"I found it after she died," Dad said. "It proved to me what I suspected was true. She found a lump in her breast and didn't do anything until it was too late."

"She died because she wanted me to grow up in Alaska?"

Dad looked like he stuck his finger in a light socket.

"Is that what you think? Is that what you've carried around all these years?" He got up and paced. He sat. Got up again. "God, will the hurt never stop coming?"

"The two of you wear me out with all the pacing you do," Carrie, always the calm and practical one, jumped in. "*Sit* and talk to Wade, Jack. How can he listen to someone that's practically running in circles?"

Dad sat on the sofa next to Carrie and across from me. "It's much more complicated than your mom wanting you to grow up in Alaska. It starts further back. Your mom's parents thought I was a fool to leave my job, uproot your mom and you to live on nothing out in the sticks. Jemma was the only one that your mother spoke to after we moved, and they fought more than anything else. She was always trying to make your mom 'get some sense in her head.' "

Carrie took one of Dad's hands in hers. Dad closed his eyes and then he looked at Carrie. There were no secrets between them. They fed each other with the long spoons.

How could I take a chance of turning the world against them again?

But how could I ever have what they had if I was untruthful all my life?

Dad's voice interrupted my thoughts. "Maybe Jemma was right. Your mother wasn't cut out for such a harsh, lonely life, but I was too selfish to see that. We argued about everything *but* Alaska. When your mom found that lump, she knew I'd take her back to Seattle, get her the care she needed. But she didn't say a word. Not to me, not to Jemma."

"I knew. I read her journal," I said.

"Did you understand what might happen if you didn't show your mother's journal to your father?" Carrie asked me.

"No," I said. Almost a whisper.

"Of course not. If you had understood that she would

die, would you have told your father and left Alaska to save your mother's life?"

"Yes. Sure, I would, but . . ."

"There are no buts," Carrie said. "You were caught in a trap and you didn't even know how you got in it."

"Carrie's right," Dad said. "I finally noticed how much weight your mom had lost and took her to the clinic, but the cancer had metastasized. The doctor didn't give her more than six months."

"I remember when we went to the clinic in Fairbanks. I thought that was such a big deal because we stayed in a hotel. Then on the way home, you and Mom told me she was sick." I stopped. "I remember her being sick for longer than six months after that."

"She died less than three months later. It felt long to you," Dad said.

"I still don't get it," I said. "Why did she let herself die rather than leave Alaska?"

Dad sighed. "She wanted us to live where I was happy. Where you would be free from city crime and enjoy the last frontier. But, Wade, some of it was sheer hardheadedness. She wouldn't let her parents win their argument. She'd die first. And she did."

His voice got uneven. "I was furious with her for so long. She could have saved herself. I felt like she cheated us."

"I was mad at her, too. For a long time. But I finally got over it," I said.

"When?"

"When I figured out that Carrie loved me. I forgave Mom for dying then."

"That's what did it for me, too," Dad said.

That night Dad and I needed a lot of coffee and a lot of tissues. Carrie needed her share, too. But I was bursting through and over the big breakers, sailing against the wind, landing with a hard thump, but landing on the smoother water on the other side.

The night I finished writing, there was slow rolling thunder and soft steady rain. I wrapped the books in my poncho and walked to Sam's in shorts and a tee, letting myself soak in the stuff like a shower. I opened my mouth and drank. It was clean and warm and new.

I knocked, gave Sam the books, asked her to read them, and left.

I was done.

I had begun.

What would happen?

I stood at the waterline, letting the wave nuzzle my feet. It didn't matter. I would . . .

Live with it.

Chapter 29
LIVING WITH IT

I closed the cover of the last book and grabbed my laptop. Searched the archives. Fairbanks Daily News-Miner. *First article reports two children in a fire. Both hospitalized. Both names withheld until details are known. Second article. One boy seriously burned. One boy catatonic but physically unhurt. Boy's father treated for burns to hands and arms. Third article. Burned boy identified as Bobby Clarke. Died of burns. Other boy remains unidentified. Troopers believe he poured gasoline on Clarke and set the fire. Unidentified child's father tried to save Clarke. Perpetrator still unresponsive.*

Another article with a picture of a burned cabin. CABIN FIRE VIGILANTE JUSTICE? the headline read.

I moved forward to the editorials when Wade/Kip was put in a mental hospital for juvenile offenders. Most of Alaska was outraged.

This was getting me nowhere. I knew all this. Well, at least it told me that Wade was truthful in his narrative.

How much of a chance did I want to take? Could I do this? I Googled a name. Still there. I punched the number into my cell, hesitated, then hit SEND.

"Hello."

A woman.

"Hello," I said. I should have thought about what to say. "I . . . uh, is this the mother of . . . Bobby Clarke?"

"Who is this?" Her voice cracked, teary and angry in a quick swirl.

"You don't know me, but—I . . . what I want to know is . . . what you can tell me about Kip McFarland?"

There was silence. I couldn't even hear her breathing. But before she spoke I felt it — the hate had no trouble traveling the thousands of miles to fill my ear.

"He's a vicious little bastard that burned my baby to death, that's what I can tell you. And he walked off and lives his life somewhere like he didn't do a thing."

The pain caught up with the hate then, I think. She made hiccuping sounds. I realized they were sobs she tried to hold in, sobs that refused to be held back. She almost whimpered when she said, "He didn't even go to prison. Like burning my boy wasn't worth . . ."

She pulled in a deep, hard breath and pulled out the hate she needed to keep talking. "Faked some kind of craziness. Crazy like a fox. Four years. Four years he was pampered in a hospital and then they give him a new name and a free plane ride to who knows where. He's living the good life while my baby screamed his life out for three days and died."

Those brutal hiccuping sounds came back. I waited.

"There's no chance it was an accident?"

"Accident?" Now her voice grew low, conspiratorial.

"That boy was evil, clean through. His father, too. Let his wife die rather than take her to a doctor for her cancer. If the state had the death penalty, those two should have been the first."

Silence again. No sounds of crying. I still wanted to know what Wade was like before —

Her voice was sharp when she interrupted my thoughts. "You didn't say who you were or why you wanted to know about Kip McFarland. Do you know where they are? Do you? There's some besides me and my husband that think some home-style justice could still be served. Where you calling from?"

I clicked off.

Dear God. Wade and his family were still being hunted. The danger was not only from within but from without.

I Googled another subject. Child killers. What makes them kill? How many kill again? What makes the difference?

And that seemed to come down to one thing. Conscience. Does the killer have one? Do they feel remorse?

Is remorse the same thing as shame? I have shame, but

I don't really have remorse. Is remorse not forgiving yourself? I had given Wade a lot of words about acceptance. That I wouldn't trade my mistakes.

But is that true? If so, I'd have been in church. I'd have gone back to school. I wouldn't be a hermit on this beach. I wouldn't believe, deep where I won't look, that Dad and Mom are ashamed of me. That ease in myself is the mask I wear.

Does Wade wear a mask? Will he ever set someone on fire again? No. I believe that right down to my bones. Remorse runs his life. Will I ever drink again? I want a drink now. Which one of us is closer to letting their demons overtake them?

I felt safe with Wade. Accepted. That with his help, I might deal with those things that I had buried deep. But if I accept Wade, am I saying I don't deserve better than a murderer? Someone who was locked up for years? I only hurt myself, but he killed a child.

I only hurt myself? Bullshit. Look at my parents.

But if I go to Wade, am I clutching another of the walking wounded? Two fractured people hoping to make one whole? Won't that stop us from ever being strong enough on our own?

He killed a child.

I'm not strong enough to be around someone working through something this big.

He killed a child.

He was a child when he killed a child.

Maybe only two people that have hurt themselves so badly can help each other?

He set a child, a CHILD, on fire.

Walking next to him, people couldn't point one finger at us — we wouldn't know which of us they pointed at. They'd get two for the price of one. Why open myself up for that?

I can't think. I can't stop crying.

I shut down the computer, closed the books. And then shoved them under the bed.

Friday afternoon I went for a sail. Alone. Without Sam. The porpoises didn't show to keep me company either. I hadn't heard from Sam in five days. I tried not to think about her as *Elton* glided along a gentle onshore breeze. I guess she had read my story. I hadn't seen her. Her car hadn't moved from her drive. She was making it clear that she wanted no part of me. But Dad or Carrie had no complaints at work. There weren't any headlines, vicious phone calls, no hate mail. I thought Sam would let them stay safe, but this was my last sail anyway.

I pulled onto the beach when the sun was touching the horizon. The tops of the water were the color of mermaid scales. I ran the sails down and took them to the shed. I'd wash them out tomorrow morning, maybe before I left. I already had a bus ticket to Dallas. I never wanted to see water again. Dad said he'd help with an apartment. I could finish my school stuff and get into a junior college. I'd be fine. I grabbed my cell phone in the shed.

I went back out to the boat and stood beside it. The stays clanked against the mast. The sun was gone.

My phone rang.

I couldn't breathe.

It rang again.

I reached for it.

Flipped it open.

Sam.

I punched the button.

I didn't say hello. I couldn't.

"I'm here," she said. "Standing right behind you."

ACKNOWLEDGEMENTS

So many good people took care of me during the writing of this book. If anyone can make gold out of straw, it's Andrea Spooner. Jill Dembowski makes sure I send Andrea the straw. Scott Treimel tells me to use better straw. Deb Vanasse sorts the moldly straw out and tells me to shape up. Jim has to live with all that messy straw and sometimes finds just the right piece for me to use on just the right day. Victoria Stapleton never lets me get too big for my britches. An author might put words on the page; other people make it a book.

My thanks to Ajahn Pannadhammo and to Ajahn Kusalo for the quote used about the Hungry Ghosts taken from the Wheel of Life.

You may find more interesting material on their Web site and blogs:

Web site:

http://www.arrowriver.ca

Blogs:

http://bhikkhublog.blogspot.com/

www.buddhamind.info/leftside/actives/w-o-life.htm